The Magnificent Guitar of
Jorge Morel
A Life of Music

by John McClellan
and Dejan Bratić

Foreword by David Russell and Pepe Romero

1 2 3 4 5 6 7 8 9 0

This page has been left blank at the authors' request.

CONTENTS

FOREWORD

One of the most fortunate things in my life is to know Jorge Morel for so many years. We met as very young men and from the start, I have admired and loved both the musician and the person; for in Jorge they are one and the same. Music has always flowed from his heart through his guitar and through his compositions capturing the listener in a very profound way. Jorge has the ability to feel and to express the full range of emotions of humanity in a way that only those touched by genius can do. It is with complete love, admiration, and spirit of brotherhood that I congratulate Jorge Morel from the bottom of my soul.

Pepe Romero

Dear readers,

Words can only hint at the excitement that Jorge transmits in his performances.

During his concert, his personality overflows in every passage he plays, and he draws you into his music just as a magician draws a child into his conjuring act. We are beguiled by his guitar playing and can only give in to him and enjoy the musical journey through which he is guiding us.

He is a performer who grows in stature and projection in a way I have seldom seen.

When I first met him in London, I was already aware of his playing through bootleg recordings of concerts. I remember especially his rendition of "Misionera" and his beautiful "Danza in E minor." He was also captivating with "Romance Criollo" and his famous "Danza Brasilera."

He was very generous with his music and let me see everything he had with him at the time. I was immediately interested in playing some of his compositions. He had an unpublished (at that time) "Sonatina," which I loved and have included in many concerts since then. The "Sonatina" was perhaps his most "Classical" composition up till then, and it served, both for the classical players and also for Jorge, to make a bridge between the more popular music of South and North America, and the classical repertoire.

Jorge's life is an extraordinary tour through the world of music in which he lived. He tells the stories of his life, encounters with musical characters and of, at times, hilarious situations, which he recounts with humour and always with respect. His humanity and warmth are revealed as we get to know him through his own words.

Now read on and enjoy El Maestro Jorge Morel.

David Russell

PREFACE

The life of Jorge Morel [*born Jorge Scibona*] reads like a screenplay taken from a Hollywood movie. He began his life as the son of the noted Sicilian-Argentinean actor, Domingo Scibona, who encouraged young Jorge both to play the guitar and to love life and people. Through his travels, Jorge met the love of his life, Olga, and moved to New York where his artistic life flourished.

The Magnificent Guitar of Jorge Morel: A Life of Music is more than a biography of an artist; it is a story of love, loss and happiness. As Jorge says, "One should love his friends and family, drink good wine, and play good music! These are the keys to a long and happy life!"

Maestro Morel is a legend. His place in history is secured along with other greats of the guitar: Sor, Tarrega and Barrios. Within these pages, a closer look into this trailblazing legacy will reveal a remarkable crossroads where musical bravado and poetic integrity intersect. He represents a dying breed of artists: those who put heart ahead of clinical expression. To quote Shakespeare's *Hamlet*, "(We) shall not look upon his like again."

It is indeed our privilege to call Jorge Morel our friend and to honor both his creativity and his life with this work.

John McClellan and Deyan Bratić
January 24, 2007

ACKNOWLEDGEMENTS

John would like to thank...

Jorge. As a young man, I used to spend hours listening to your records. Never did I dream we would become friends! I have such great admiration for your character of integrity, passion, and love. I feel humbled by the honor in working on this book with you. It is long overdue!

Jorge's daughter, Francesca Scibona, for her enthusiasm and the great photos of her mom and dad. I also wish to extend my gratitude to Maurice Summerfield, and, to Bertram Photography for providing some terrific photographs of Jorge for this book. Additional thanks to Jeffrey Herzlich for the photo used on the front cover, among other photos contributed throughout.

The Bratić family, for their friendship in hosting Jorge during his stay in St. Louis this summer. I know he became a part of their family during his visit, and their generosity made our work with Jorge possible.

I would like offer special thanks to Dan Dreyfus and his staff photographer, Julie Birkemeier, of Dreyfus & Associates Photography. Dan has been a true friend over the years, and very generous in his support of the various projects that seem to be constantly in the works. He and his staff have contributed countless hours restoring many of the old photographs that Jorge had entrusted to us. The success of this book will ultimately owe much to the efforts and kindness of this man. I know he worked hard because of our friendship and because of his desire to honor Jorge.

Lastly, without my collaborator and friend, Deyan Bratić, this project would still be a dream. He worked tirelessly to make this book a reality. It is impossible for me to thank him enough for all of his hard work and dedication to this endeavor. In the words of Jorge, "You're amazing!"

Deyan would like to thank...

My father and mother, Rocko and Sandra, whose support and belief in me have remained the bedrock throughout my life. If one is fortunate enough to be blessed with such a gift, one must never lose sight of it. The perils that often accompany the types of labor required for a project as this do not always imprint positively on one's own mind and general well-being. Their undying love and patience has helped deliver me through years of seclusion and a relentless work ethic. On many levels, it must be recognized that their contribution to this book is far too invaluable to justly acknowledge here. Bereft of it, my offering within these pages simply would not be possible. I love you.

My friend and co-conspirator, John McClellan. Our partnership has risen to the ideal, and he has consistently provided me support and encouragement in my endeavors. Without his vision, inexhaustible creativity and passion, this book, like our other works, would remain an unrealized sketch at best.

And... I would also like to thank the man himself: Jorge Morel. Although people can love and appreciate the level of artistry he has so consistently exuded throughout his exemplary career, perhaps what deserves greater emphasis is that he is a true pinnacle of generosity, kindness, and virtue that is seldom found in people these days. Furthermore, with the time and assistance he has given this undertaking, he has endowed both John and me with a great luxury: the confidence to declare emphatically that the music presented in this work is—to use the Maestro's oft-repeated phrase: *"The real McCoy!"*

From Jorge

I would like to say a few words about John McClellan,

I want to express my gratitude to this talented man and say that I am happy and honored to be his friend. I was also very happy when he asked me sometime ago if he and his friend could write a book about my life and music career. Well, here it is, and it is wonderful, especially coming from a man who can play the instrument so well; it is a great feeling.

…and Deyan Bratić,

John's partner on this book. When John introduced me to this young man and I watched him work with my music on the computer, I was very impressed with the quality and care he put into his work. He is also an accomplished guitarist and has a deep understanding of the instrument. I am very lucky to have this talented young man working on this book.

Thank you, John and Deyan, for a very fine book, and your friendship.

Jorge

Photo courtesy of Jim McLaughlin © 2006

Photo courtesy of Bertram Photography © 2002

JORGE MOREL: AN APPRECIATION

It has been said that the guitar, with its feminine contours, allows facility for caress and is therefore the most romantic, if not intimate of musical instruments.

If so, then Jorge Morel might well be described as the guitar's most ardent lover.

Witness him perform, and you will immediately detect the intimacy, passion, and spirit that emanates from his fervent embrace of the instrument to which he has unstintingly dedicated an entire lifetime.

I believe that no other guitarist of the classical genre matches this extraordinarily loving relationship. And it is one considerably enhanced not just by Morel's vibrant, pulsating compositions proudly evoking the melodic and rhythmic traditions of his native Argentina, but by the incredible power, panache, strength, skill and fluency of his playing.

In that loving embrace, Jorge is, at once, both husband, father and child of the guitar—father through faithful guardianship and unwavering tutelage; and child through the unbridled excitement and innocent joy flowing from fingers untouched by time's rigors to the heart and soul of his audiences.

We, who have had the privilege of savoring his well–seasoned virtuosity from close range, can only marvel at the amazing rhythmic textures that integrate with his uniquely mesmeric melodic inventions cascading like illuminating silver pearls of musical wisdom experience up and down the fretboard.

And often at lightning speed!

Afterward, we can only bow before the altar of a rare musical genius that delivers incredible strength and poignancy of performance—unsullied, undiluted, and undiminished by a rambunctious, obstreperous age, forever threatening.

Beethoven once claimed that music was a higher revelation than philosophy and in this Argentinean virtuoso's capable hands, that musical truth is readily apparent, and always confirmed. What we hear in his playing is the quintessence of a Morelian musical classicism—uniquely transcendent; resplendent in its clarity and depth in terms of the guitar's sonorous versatility; and advancing music's most revelatory powers.

All, of course, made possible by a humble six–stringed instrument that invites embrace and to which grand guitar maestro Jorge Morel faithfully responds with spiritual zeal—and magnanimous affection—for a very grateful world.

Long may he continue to whet our appetites for the truly extraordinary in classical guitar composition and performance.

Vince Moran

Honeymooning in Honolulu, 1961.

Honolulu, Hawaii: 1961—I don't remember when exactly. I was playing in a club there, a beautiful place. *Down the Beach Combers* was the name of the club. I was just married to my wife Olga, and we went together. That was really our honeymoon. I was booked for four weeks, but we stayed for seven. The owner of the place seemed to like me. He said, "Jorge, if you want to stay, you're welcome." Seven weeks in Hawaii! One evening was special because they told me Frank Sinatra was coming in from somewhere to make a movie. He was stopping in with a group of people.

My wife and I were very excited. I said, "Well, tonight I'm going to do the show that I usually do," because they had all the people there. I did two shows every night. So here comes Frank Sinatra with thirty to thirty-five people—a big table. Now, this was 1961, so Frank Sinatra was a fairly young man.

I was playing when he came in with these people, so I stopped for a while and tuned the guitar to let all of them sit at their table. They called my wife, and I remember she was wearing a Hawaiian moo-moo dress. They said, "Sit with Mr. Sinatra and his friends." My wife was thrilled, of course. Now, I was onstage and I see this table right in front of me; I was very nervous. I thought, "What do I play? Okay, I'll play my show." I played a couple of pieces, and then came the applause. "Beautiful! Beautiful!" Then comes this request from Mr. Sinatra for "Laura." I learned later that he had been talking to my wife and asked, "What is his favorite piece?" And she said, "'Laura.'" In those days, I loved that piece. So Frank Sinatra says,

"Hey, Jorge, can you play 'Laura?'" I said,

"Yeah!" So I played "Laura." I thought, 'Oh, my gosh!!' because he recorded that so beautifully. He liked it. After that, he asked,

"Can you play flamenco?" Frank Sinatra is asking *me* to play flamenco. So I said,

"Mr. Sinatra, I am sorry. I don't play flamenco." He said,

"*Fake* it!"

He knew I was Latin American and that I played some Spanish music during my forty-five minute show. To play for forty-five minutes, I was worried that people would get up from their tables, walk out, and smoke a cigarette or something. But when he said that, I played "Mosaico Española," which was like a medley of Spanish music. I even played *Capriccio espagnol* by Rimsky-Korsakov. I also played "Granada," because this was all music that I was playing at the time. Maybe I played "Carioca," who knows? After I played all of this, they went crazy! So Frank said, "Oh, gorgeous! Beautiful!" I don't know if he knew flamenco. I don't think he did. Flamenco is something *special*.

This story is a lovely one to me, because it is the only time I met Sinatra, and I am one of his greatest fans. I still have his records, and I listen to a radio program in New York done by a guy named Jonathan Schwartz. He has a weekend show, Saturdays and Sundays from noon until 7:00 on WNYC. He plays Sinatra fifty percent of the time. And I'm there. I am *there*!

Jorge's mother and father in Buenos Aires, Argentina, 1929

MY HERITAGE

Buenos Aires is a city of many European people who came from Italy, Spain, and Germany. They worked very hard to build the country. Buenos Aires is like a European city in the middle of South America, like Madrid with a little bit of Paris and a little bit of London, all in one city.

I came from an Italian family. My grandparents came from Sicily at the end of the nineteenth century. My father was born in 1903 and my mother in 1909, both in the same neighborhood, so they knew each other from a very early age. My mother was a refined, beautiful lady who loved my father very much, and he loved her too. My mother had to put up with him many times because of his difficult career [actor]. We all would travel with him—my mother, brother, and me. But my parents got along very well; I do remember this.

Unfortunately, my mother passed away at a very young age, in 1946. This left the responsibility on my father to care for my brother and me. His work made it difficult for him to stay with us. He needed somebody. He remarried and his new wife gave me my sister, Cristina. Soon after that, his new wife passed away also. After this, he decided to remain unmarried for the rest of his life.

Brother Osvaldo, friend Roberto, Jorge, and sister, Cristina
Buenos Aires, 1985.

In concert with the Velázquez guitar he gave to Chet Atkins.

I had a 1970 Fleta guitar. Ignacio Fleta sent it to me. I ordered it from him in 1967, and I remember going to the airport with my brother to pick it up. That guitar was a real treasure! The reason I stopped playing that guitar was that it had problems. It was a delicate instrument and it cracked. The bridge came off, and Manuel Velázquez re-glued it. Then the fingerboard cracked and warped. I remember leaving the guitar with Chet [*Atkins*] for an entire day, and he used a hot iron to straighten the fingerboard. He fixed it!

My first guitar was from the Casa Nuñez, a Spanish luthier in Buenos Aires. I think his shop is closed now. The luthier's name was Diego Grazia, and he was a wonderful person as was the guitar. The guitar was built in 1938, and it was in excellent shape and sounded beautiful. This was my first good guitar until a guy in Cuba changed the top and ruined it. The man took the soul from my guitar and it was never the same. I brought it to the United States and eventually sold it to one of my students. If that guitar had been in its original condition, I would have never sold it! It was my father's first gift to me.

When I went to Puerto Rico, I had to acquire a new guitar. I cannot remember the luthier's name, but it is the guitar I used on the Decca recordings. Later, I ordered a guitar from Germany by a builder named Edgar Monch, and then after I settled here in the United States, I met Manuel Velázquez. I have owned three Velázquez guitars. The third guitar was the one I gave to Chet Atkins.

What did you like about the Velázquez guitar?

I liked the tone. When you look for a powerful guitar, Manuel Velázquez is not the man! My Fleta was not a very loud guitar either. But the Velázquez had a magical G string. That sound—I thought I was playing something from heaven! The G string sounded like a cello. When you played a chord, each note was so balanced.

That is the key to a great guitar: a defined G string with a singing first string.

The G string is important, mostly because it comes after the fourth string, which is wound. The jump from the D to the G—it is a different world! A good G string really helps. My new guitar was built by Richard DiCarlo. He gave me this guitar! It has wonderful clarity and all the qualities I just described.

After the Velázquez came the Fleta and eventually a Ramirez. I purchased this guitar from James Sherry in Chicago in 1970, and it was very big: 665mm! It was like playing on a tree! [*laughs*] The sound was great but I suffered playing that guitar. I punished myself for years trying to play that guitar.

What is your preference in scale length?

I prefer 650 or 655 milimeters: these seem to be the standard scale lengths that are popular these days. Velázquez built a great fingerboard; it was the most comfortable fingerboard I have ever played. Then he started building even smaller and shorter scale length guitars.

I finally sold my Ramirez because I started having problems with it as I did with the Fleta. The finish had thousands of cracks. I traveled from Canada all the way to Puerto Rico, and that guitar could not stand the differences in climates. I had a student who said, "If you ever want to sell the Ramirez, let me know!" So…I let him know! [*laughs*]

After the Ramirez, I played a guitar by Dieter Hopf. I came to this guitar through my friend Tony Acosta. I played this guitar when I went to Poland in the 1980s. It is also the guitar I used when I filmed all the Mel Bay videos. Eventually I started playing a guitar made by John Price. Tony started promoting his guitars about 4 or 5 years ago. Tony said, "Jorge, listen to this guitar!" When I picked it up, I almost fell down! I said, "I can't lift it!" When I played it, I loved the sound!

If someone came to you and they possessed the power to build the perfect guitar, which of course does not exist, what would characterize your 'perfect' guitar?

My perfect guitar is the one I feel most comfortable playing. It must suit your type of playing; the approach of the right hand. All of us are different. Some guitarists play loud; some try to play like Julian Bream, with a softer touch but with many colors. John Williams is completely different from Bream, or Pepe or Angel Romero…wow!

When I play fast scales, I need a responsive guitar that suits my technique. More importantly, I need a guitar that possesses the ability to sound good playing my music and arrangements.

It is a guitar with a quick response and a transparency.

With my new DiCarlo, the separation of the notes when you play a scale: nothing is lost. When you play the bass, it sustains so beautifully. The basses are not booming, because that is no good. You play a bass string and you have to stop it like a pedal.

Sort of the difference between a bass sonority and baritone sonority.

Richard DiCarlo came to my house for a dinner party. He asked me to try his new guitar. Then he said, "Happy birthday Jorge, it is yours!"

Is it cedar or spruce?

It is cedar. It has eight little holes on the side: little sound ports. I am hard of hearing, but this new guitar is so easy for me to hear. [*Ed. Note: Earlier in his life, Morel suffered an injury to his eardrum.*] So many people do not like this design. Robert Ruck came up with this innovation, and for me it is great!

I love cedar top guitars; they have a more elegant sound to me. Spruce takes too long to mature, but cedar is good right away. If a cedar guitar is not good from the first five to six months, forget it! It is no good!

I like normal-sized frets. I don't like big frets, because then the glissandos hurt my fingers. I like my frets rounded and not too high. I also like wider string spacing at the nut. Most luthiers make the spacing at the nut too close together. I prefer the kind of spacing used on Ramirez guitars. Whenever I get a new guitar, I usually have the spacing changed because I like more room; not too close—everybody knows that!

I think every builder likes to hear the guitar naked; nothing electronic that will interfere with the natural sound. The guitar will never be as loud as the violin. Even the banjo is louder than the guitar…no, we don't want to hear the banjo! I am not fan of this instrument!

Nor am I!

The guitar is loud enough for our use and for the music that is already written. Technology allows us to amplify if needed. John Williams uses beautiful amplification and you hear the guitar.

You know the saying, "The guitar does not sound loud but it sounds far."

Yes, exactly right!

IN ARGENTINA, WE PLAY SOCCER!

Jorge (far left), with soccer teammates, 1945.

In Argentina, soccer is the number one sport. Every boy plays soccer. Most of us played. I was not very good, but I guess I played all right. I certainly was not Diego Maradona! I loved soccer so much. This photograph with my friends was taken when I was 14 years old. My uncle was the coach. He tried to put me in but I said, "Look, Theo, I don't play very well!" The other guys on my team were great. I was out of touch with soccer a little because I was already studying the guitar. Soccer was a part of my life which ended very quickly.

I loved to kick the ball. I was a very fast runner; that is why I played right wing. I played right wing because in those days the formations in soccer were different. I was on wing because I could kick the ball far and I could run fast. I had no idea what on earth I was doing. [*laughs*] If I was a good soccer player, this would have taken me away from the guitar! I guess I made the right choice.

Jorge in concert with John McClellan and Kirk Hanser of the Hanser-McClellan Guitar Duo, 2005.

PERCUSSION NOTATION EXPLAINED

It is often remarked that rhythm is the lifeblood of music, a paramount element over which to gain mastery if one aspires to carry on the musical tradition with conviction, authenticity, and respect. In this regard, the music of Jorge Morel is *most certainly* no exception.

A great aspect of the classical guitar which he helped pioneer involves treating the guitar as a percussive instrument. This expansion of the instrument's inherent resources brings forth a plethora of new possibilities to the guitarist, possibilities that can enrich approaches to composition and arranging for what is often labeled, mistakenly, a 'limited instrument.'

Some of the pieces presented in this book, ranging from classic arrangements to brand new compositions, incorporate these percussive elements. One of the unprecedented aims for this book is to clearly define and notate the passages where such techniques are implemented, so that the musician yearning to master these passages will be able to assimilate them immediately without confusion or possibility of error. By studying the legend below, it is our hope that the guitarist attempting the pieces to follow will bask in the rewards of carrying forward the musical tradition—the lifeblood—of this Argentinean master's music.

1) RIGHT HAND thumb strikes bass side of soundboard (near soundhole).

2) RIGHT HAND thumb on the bridge.

3) RIGHT HAND tambura on the strings.

4) RIGHT HAND finger taps on face of guitar (treble side) just beneath soundhole.

5) RIGHT HAND closed fist slaps strings down above soundhole.

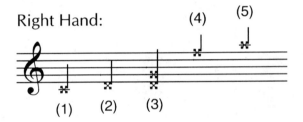

6) LEFT HAND finger taps face of guitar on upper right bout, near 14th fret (treble side).

7) LEFT HAND open hand slaps side of guitar on shoulder.

ISLAND
TV
GUIDE

Jorge Morel

NOV. 5–11

guía de TELEVISION

15¢

Dedicated to Michéle Ramo

LITTLE FANTASY

JORGE MOREL

16

Olga and Jorge. New York, 1968.

April 3, 2004

Maestro Jorge Morel, you came this great city of New York in 1961 to share your music with an audience eager for the sounds of guitar. You made an outstanding debut at Carnegie Hall to a sold out crowd, and this was to be a performance that would commence a long and prosperous career in music. 43 years later, you have given performances at Alice Tully Hall in New York, Queen Elizabeth Hall and Wigmore Hall in London, National Hall in Dublin and Suntory Hall in Tokyo. You have traveled the world far and wide to exotic locales, sharing your music with enthusiastic audiences from Argentina, Brazil, Canada, Colombia, Cuba, Ecuador, Puerto Rico, France, Holland, Italy, Norway, Poland, Scotland, Spain, Sweden, Finland, Greece, Singapore, and Germany.

But your contributions go far beyond the realm of performance. A connoisseur of the finest music around the world, you have created a unique compositional language that combines the captivating rhythms of Latin America with the enchanting harmonies of Jazz. Your enthralling melodies have spoken to millions of people. You have recorded numerous CDs for RCA, Decca, Guitar Masters, Sesac and Luthier Music. In addition to your own library of recordings, your music has been performed and recorded by some of the finest musicians in the world: John Williams, The Assad Brothers, Pepe and Angel Romero, Christopher Parkening, David Russell, David Starobin, Carlos Barbosa-Lima, Ricardo Iznaola, Eliot Fisk, Krzysztof Pelech, Hillary Fields, The Hanser McClellan Duo, The Greek Guitar Duo, and the outstanding musicians that have given their time be here tonight on this special occasion: Dennis Koster, Jorge Cabellero, the Newman and Oltman Guitar Duo, Rene Izquierdo, Elina Chekan, Joshua Bavaro, and Jason Vieaux.

You have lent your years of experience to those who seek your tutelage, passing on your knowledge to those who love guitar as you do. Students young and old find solace in your instruction, and you give the next generation your gift of music to continue the traditions that you have carried during your lifetime.

You are truly a man of the world, a man who is admired and respected around the globe for your beautiful music, your exceptional performances, your charismatic personality, your kind heart, and your complete love for music, the guitar and above all, life. You live and breathe the words you speak, and those who know you are inspired to follow their hearts and dreams and to live a life as complete and full of joy as yours.

Maestro Jorge Morel, in recognition of a lifetime of invaluable contributions to the classical guitar and its literature, it is with great honor and pleasure that the New York City Classical Guitar Society presents to you the 2004 Lifetime Achievement Award.

Sincerely,

J. Andrew Dickenson, Artistic Director

Lester S. Long, President

Ivan Gomez, Vice President

Tim Westwig, Event Coordinator

Vic Juris, Barney Kessel, Jorge, and Martin Taylor.

Dedicated to Bill Bay

STACCATO DANCE

JORGE MOREL

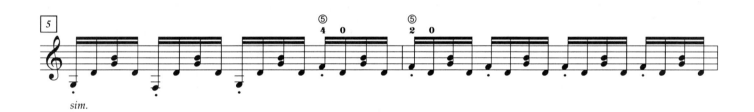

STACCATO DANCE

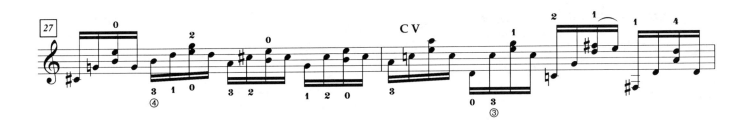

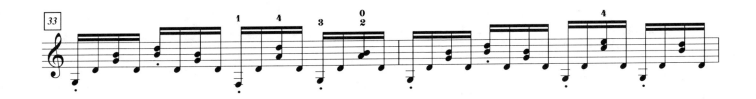

STACCATO DANCE

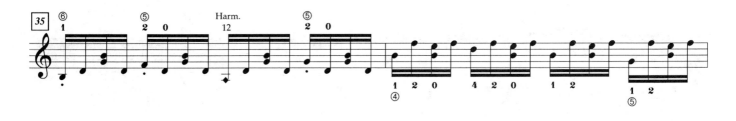

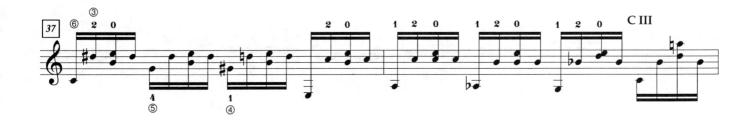

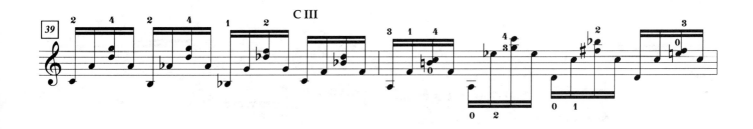

Photo courtesy of Maurice Summerfield.

PRACTICE AND TECHNIQUE

I like scales. I did not like them when I was a kid. I grew more and more to like practicing scales, especially when I played them using the rest stroke. It concerns me when I see a young guitarist play the guitar with the right hand deviated to the left [*from the player's perspective*].

The right hand should be perpendicular to the string. With proper positioning when you pluck the string, you can allow the finger to rest almost on the center of the nail on the string. Look at powerful players like John Williams, Pepe Romero or Angel Romero. The right hand is almost straight, unlike Segovia. When I see people play now, they strike the string with the right side of the nail. They cannot rest stroke. A scale without the rest stroke has no value to me; you don't play like that!

With Angel Romero, 2005.

I worry about guitarists who indiscriminately go in and out of free and rest stroke with no musical concern for articulation.

If you position your right hand too far to your left, the audience will riot! You know what I mean. The full sound comes from the center of the nail. It is impossible to feel the note without resting on the string. You must be able to bring out the melodic line. If you don't bring out the line, then you MUST play the banjo! [*laughs*]

One should practice scales with the index and middle fingers, not three fingers (index, middle, and ring). Using three fingers is for tremolo. Some people try to play fast scales using three fingers; I don't think this is good. Each finger produces a completely different sound; the balance is bad. I think index and middle is the best. I love arpeggios and campanella on the guitar. I use campanella technique in many of my pieces.

That is the perfect example of playing to the strength of the guitar. Scales were played using campanella technique in the Baroque period on the guitar and it sounds equally beautiful on the modern guitar.

Trying to make a guitar sound like a piano is a mistake, especially when arranging a piece originally written for the piano. They try to sound like a piano—forget it! Arranging Chopin for the guitar is a waste of time. Maybe a little prelude might work, but I think if you have to punish the guitar and the music, then you are going in the wrong direction.

In my opinion, you sacrifice a little of the music but *none* of the guitar. If you sacrifice the guitar for the sake of the music, then it is not going to be 'guitaristic.' The music is going to suffer anyway.

You have to ask yourself, 'What is the point?'

You have to understand a little bit of composition in order *not* to harm the music when you arrange for the guitar. The music must sound good on the guitar—forget about the piano! All sacrifices must come from the music and not the guitar because both will suffer. You have to think of the guitar ninety-five percent of the time and the music five percent.

Many guitarists play the notes but not the music. You really groove when you play. Did you practice with a metronome when you were younger?

I had a metronome because they gave it to me. I only use the metronome now to put tempo marks in my pieces; I don't practice with it. I have never used it. Rhythm grew up within me; I like rhythm. If you depend on the metronome too much and don't have the feel inside of you, take up another career. [*laughs*] A musician is *born*. When you first start to learn the guitar you need help of course, but it is obvious if the talent is there. Music is *not* for everybody.

When you hear kids play, you know some will become very good. A few, perhaps ten out of one hundred, will play, if you are lucky. Then out of those ten, only one has a *true* gift. All the others just play for fun.

I often get questions from these students asking me, "Maestro, can I make a living playing the guitar?" I don't know what to say. I don't want to lie to them, so I must be gentle and supportive. We are not magicians. Some people cannot hear, and if you cannot hear, then it is a waste of time. It is a delicate balance being a teacher.

What are your thoughts concerning players from the past up to the present?

I meet and hear many new guitarists here in New York. One is Rene Izquierdo, a very beautiful player from Cuba who teaches in Wisconsin. The other is Jorge Caballero, who possesses an extraordinary technique. But everything they play is fast because they are young. However, Rene and Jorge have the potential to go a long way.

Young guitarists should listen to Maestro Segovia, Pepe and Angel Romero, Julian Bream and duo guitarists such as you and Kirk [*Hanser-McClellan Guitar Duo*] because duo music for guitar is a great way of musical socialization. I am partial also because I love your playing!

Thank you Jorge! Kirk and I are humbled by your kindness.

When I worked at the Village Gate, I came to know Errol Garner immediately. He was playing upstairs and I was playing downstairs. I have been exposed to the greats and this was important to my development. You have to listen to all kinds of music—chamber music, orchestral, and piano.

When I began teaching students, they knew only Guiliani and Sor. I said, "There are other composers you must listen to!" They would say, "But they don't play the guitar." I tell them, "That is the point!"

If we guitarists listen to only music for the guitar, we become musically inbred.

Yes; that is why they don't play the music, they just play the guitar. They play fast and have a good tone with a great technique, but the music is not there! They need to listen to great composers, not just Bach or Mozart, but Ravel and Debussy. You must listen to all kinds of music. Then, you can play whatever you want.

A rare Colombian issued 78 record, 1959.

"Jorge was one of my guitar heroes when I was a little boy growing up in Cuba."
—Manuel Barrueco

Performing for daughter Francesca, 1999.

DANZA DE MAYO

JORGE MOREL

DANZA DE MAYO

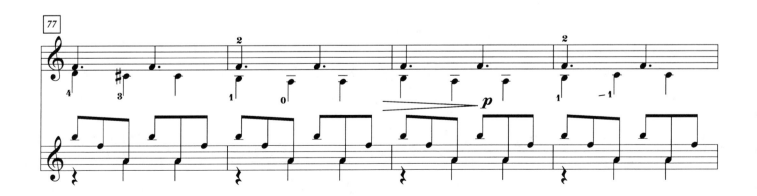

*Jorge performing with John McClellan at a tribute concert
for Chet Atkins in St. Louis, 2002.*

MY BROTHER

The first guitar my father gave me was a nice-sounding guitar. One day I was practicing and my brother was in the bedroom with me. I was playing and playing—he told me something and I was not paying attention. Then I said something that hurt him. He said, "What?" I repeated myself. He picked up a heavy shoe with a wooden heel and threw it at me. I instinctively held the guitar in front of my face to protect myself. Needless to say, it cracked my guitar. My father was furious with us. We were just doing what brothers do!

With brother Osvaldo in Buenos Aires, 1989.

Tony is my best friend. He is a great businessman but, most importantly, he loves my music! It is a great feeling when you have someone who really believes in you, in your music and your art. We all need help, as most musicians do not have much money. I am not complaining; I am always trying to better my life.

My relationship with Tony goes back over twenty-five years. His business, Luthier Music Corporation, makes strings, sells guitars, books, and all things associated with guitar. When we met, he was my student. We became friends and his goal was to operate a business that promoted the guitar because he loves it so much.

Brother Osvaldo, Tony, and son, Jorge, 1984.

Jorge with Tony (left), Gene Bertoncini, and Maurice Summerfield.

Jorge performing in a play. Buenos Aires, 1950.

THE STORY OF MOREL

I left Argentina in October of 1957. Two to five years before that, a young lady, who use to be an actress with my father in the company, and I were very good friends. This lady, Rosalinda Ricatti, Italiano, a beautiful, good actress said, "Jorge, maybe we can change your name 'Scibona.'" This was because nobody could pronounce that name well. People would say, "Ski–bona." I said, "I don't know…if you want. I have no ideas. Which name?" So she came back with a book and said, "Hey, I've got a name for you: 'Morel!'" I said, "Well, why not? 'Jorge Morel.'" Morel is a French name. And that was it.

The thing is, this young lady dies two years later of a heart attack. She was twenty-eight or twenty-nine years old. A gorgeous girl, so beautiful she was. Her mother went to wake her up in the morning—like every morning. Her nickname was 'Chuchi.' "Hey, Chuchi! Wake up! It's nine-o-clock." She didn't. "Hey! Come on, the coffee is ready." She never woke up; she was gone. That is a sad, incredible story.

She had given me that name, and I felt so bad when she passed because we were good friends and she was such a lovely lady. After this, I felt so close to that name and I thought, 'I am going to keep that name.' And believe me, there was no other kind of relationship with her; we were just friends. But I kept the name, in her memory. It's not my own name, but…

I was devastated because we were so close. My father *suffered*. And *her mother*, an old lady, outlived her daughter by another ten years at least. She was a good actress, too. We visited her mother until she died. But that was it; that was the story of Morel. Where the hell did Morel come from?

"I believe that people do not know how to listen anymore. I really believe that, and I'm afraid of the future of music."

Radio, for me, at this time I would say is *more* important than television. I used to listen to radio before, because we didn't have television in Argentina. Now, I am getting really tired of television. I don't think they are getting any new ideas; I think they've ran out of gas. Television has become a very commercial-type of thing. I see things and think that, not only do I not like it, but am *afraid* that *this* is the direction that television is going to go. Look at the Grammy Awards. It is a program that takes about two hours, and you look at these shows they present. These guys…why do they dress like that?! Why do they act and talk like that?! This is not even English! Now, I am not a conservative, but I really think that this is the wrong way to go. If this is the Grammys for the future, you can have it. I am glad that David Russell won, since my music is there, but I really don't care. I really think that, if this is the way that it's going to go, unless it takes a different direction. The culture? This is not the way I want to see it. I don't want anything bad for these people. Let them have it—I don't want anything to do with it. Because it is getting *uglier*, and *louder*. I am a guitarist, and maybe the instrument talks for me. I don't know.

What is good music? Can you tell me what *good* music is? Do you like rap? You know that rap is rhythm. Well, yes, there are lyrics, if they want to call it that. Whatever they are saying, I don't understand. It's rhythm mostly. Okay, I am a Latin American man—a white man—whose been living in New York for forty-three years. This is not about race to me, not that I am covering myself. I love Wynton Marsalis. This is a man that I really like. He's a talented man, and you know what he said about rap? "I'm ashamed." He *said* that!

I'm not against that kind of music, if you want to call it music. But the Grammy Awards, this television show where people spend millions of dollars for a thirty second advertisement—an incredible amount of money—is a show that takes more than fifty percent of the time for what? Rap, and rock. Now, what about jazz, which is the essence of American music? I'm not talking about Gershwin and Ellington. These guys are gone, but they are still here, and they will be here forever. We all play Duke Ellington and Gershwin. *None* of these 'new' guys are ever going to come even *close* to the incredible talent of these people. I am saying this here, I'll say it on CBS, or ABC, or NBC. If you want me tomorrow, I'll go on network and I'll say that. I am not afraid of losing anything, because I don't *have* anything to lose.

I believe that people do not know *how* to listen anymore. I really believe that, and I am afraid of the future of music. I'm a guitarist, and I'm afraid of the future of the guitar. Where is it going to go? The versatility of the artist is the guitar itself, because the guitar is a versatile instrument to begin with. Take the guitar and analyze it: the origin of the guitar, the history. Who played the guitar first? Where did it come from? Guitarists today really don't care about that—they don't take the *time*.

Photo courtesy of Maurice Summerfield.

JUGUETEANDO

from *Guitar Moods*

SMC 1110 NY (1966)

JORGE MOREL

51

D.S. al Coda

Coda

Repeat percussion vamp until fade out.

Written in Buenos Aires in 1955 before I left Argentina—actually one year before I left. "American Fantasy" was a piece I played every night in clubs and concerts. In those days, the city government put live performers in movie houses.

We had hundreds of movie houses in Buenos Aires, and each house was required to hire live musicians. I was playing five days a week, for several movie houses. In between movies, they put on an hour of live music between the feature films. The audiences loved it. When the musicians played, it was a nice change of pace. That gave me work for about a year. "American Fantasy" was one of the pieces I played every night during that year. I've always loved jazz, and thought this would sound good on the classical guitar.

AMERICAN FANTASY

from *The Warm Guitar of Jorge Morel*

Decca DL 74167 (1962)

JORGE MOREL

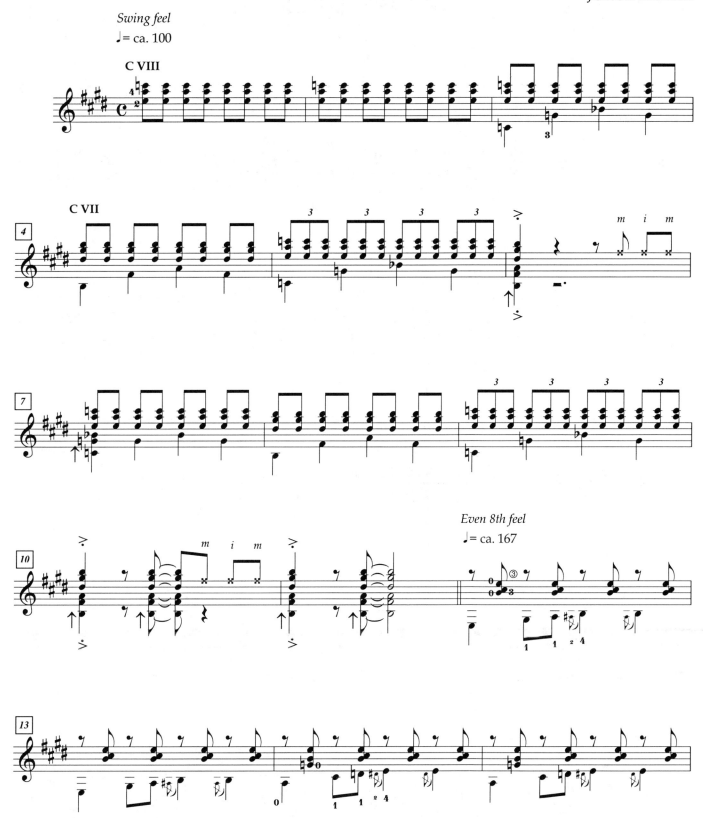

1961

Photo courtesy by Jim McLaughlin © 2005

2005

I am not good, technologically speaking, when it comes to what types of microphones are good to use. I have an engineer that lives upstairs from me who records me. He gets a beautiful sound. I don't pay attention to microphones; that is his job. I sit there, play, and then listen to whether I like the sound or not.

My process for preparing to record is simple: I don't play the piece very much, because if you don't have it by then, forget it! When you record, you are going to play the piece four or five times. Some people are lucky to get it on the first shot! I am not so lucky! I don't like to edit too much.

The thing is to have the piece fresh when you are ready to record. Just run through it a couple of times, play a scale or arpeggio—the things that make up that piece. Don't play the piece too much! Then when you record the piece, it will have more flavor, more spontaneity. It is like preparing for a concert: if you play it repeatedly, when you go to the hall you are going to play a boring recital. Just go over things slowly in the dressing room; this reinforces the memory. When you go to the stage or in front of the microphone to record the piece, it is going to come out with more fire and excitement! You want to *play* that piece!

I just put my finger on this the other day. When I listen to your recordings, I hear the spontaneity that comes from all your live playing.

It is energy, first. In those days, I was younger and I wanted to play so much! If I played a piece like "Misionera" three or four times, when you get in front of the microphone and the guys says, "You're on!" then the piece does not come with energy. You must save energy for that moment!

When I listen to *The Warm Guitar of Jorge Morel*, it sounds like everything is recorded in one take.

In those days, many of the takes did happen in one shot! I often think, 'How come I can't do that now?' Well, there is a reason for that: it's forty years later! [*laughs*]

Maybe it was the ignorance of youth. You were not thinking about the pressure of recording. Now your life experiences come into play.

I was in my late twenties. Those Decca recordings sound like a live concert. It does not sound like I was in a recording studio. Sometimes I expect applause at the end of each piece on those records!

There is so much to think about when you record. What about the quality of the sound...worrying about making too many boo-boos? I think some of my recordings are not very clean; [there are] a whole bunch of them that are not perfectly played. With energy and spontaneity, it does not matter if a few notes are not perfectly articulated. What drives me is the performance. In front of the microphone you are empty; you are alone. Guitarists are the loneliest players on the earth. You are playing without anybody being there except the guy behind the glass. You think, 'What would happen if I played like this in a hall?'

When Kirk [Hanser, of the Hanser-McClellan Guitar Duo] and I recorded "Millennium Duet," we brought a group of university students into the studio as a live audience to inspire us to play well.

Once you start playing in front of people, you gain energy from them. It can make you nervous too!

When you played with us last year at the Sheldon Concert Hall, Kirk was sitting up in the balcony with a group of university guitar students. As you were performing, they all were in awe. Kirk

leaned forward and asked them, "How does it feel to have you're ass kicked by a 74 year-old man?!" You owned the audience that night.

[*laughs*] That is funny!

Kirk came back stage and told me that. I about fell out of my chair laughing! Jorge, there is fine line between being an entertainer and an artist. What are your thoughts about this?

People should see that you care. I am there because I care about playing for you! Not only because they are paying me, [though] sometimes not enough! [*laughs*]

There is honesty in your playing which I also hear in Chet Atkins; you two have this in common. People instinctively understand this when they hear you.

Chet was unique, one of a kind, because of that honesty he projected when he played and when he spoke. I heard him play many times here in New York and in Nashville. We were very close friends. Being an artist, a true artist demands honesty.

Photo courtesy of Maurice Summerfield.

The spirit of the creative soul is restless, always striving for perfection. Such spirit possesses Jorge Morel, constantly honing and refining his arrangements and compositions. During our time with him proofing the music for this book, Jorge initially expressed great hesitance towards including *both* his Decca and RCA recorded versions of Fernando Bustamante's "Misionera." Fortunately, we have persuaded him to realize the scholastic and historical significance of presenting the two versions in this book, side-by-side. Our aim is to illustrate precisely that true art cannot be restrained: it is always changing.

When studying the two differing takes on this classic arrangement, one can easily observe Jorge's style being kindred to the spontaneity of the jazz musician's approach, much more than the premeditated and overly rehearsed method on which the classical guitarist depends. His inherent lack of complacency is merely an extension of his humble nature, as he will always downplay the relevance of old ideas in light of new discoveries. It is our belief, for all true intents and purposes of this book, that a duality must be reached. One should not only appreciate his forward-mindedness, but also bear witness to the growth of this artist from his roots. By doing so, we all can only stand enriched by his restless example.

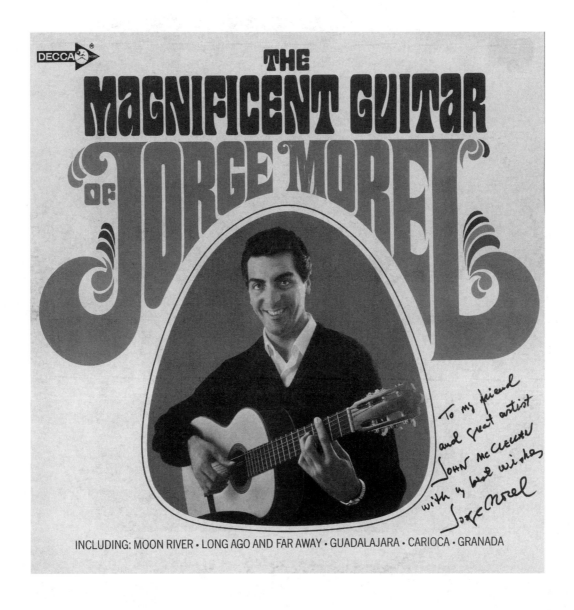

MISIONERA

from *The Magnificent Guitar of Jorge Morel*

Decca DL 4966 (1963)

FERNANDO BUSTAMANTE
arr. JORGE MOREL

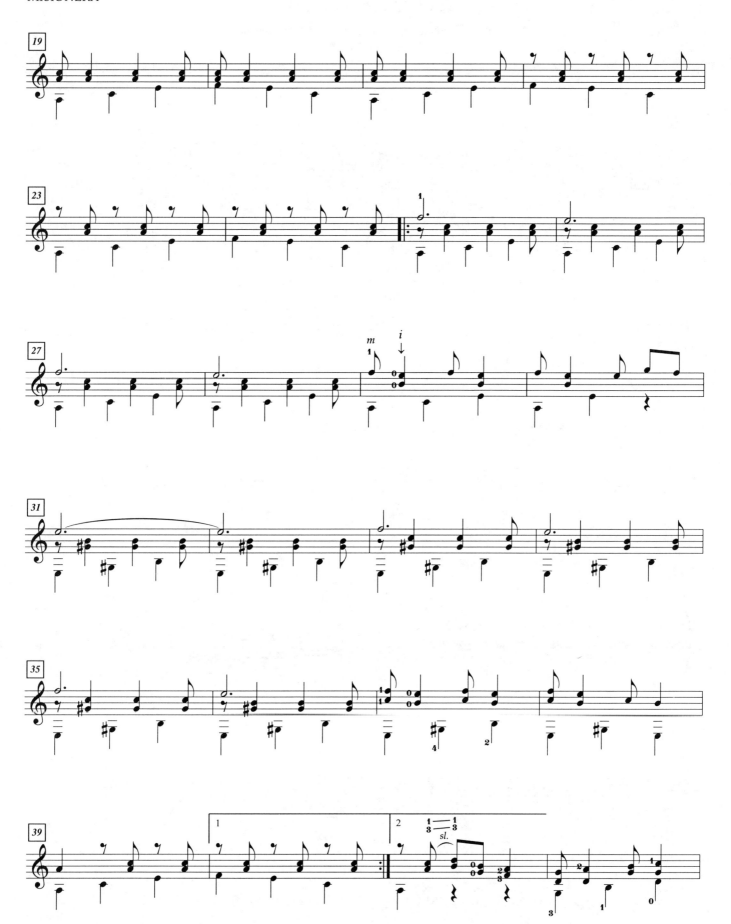

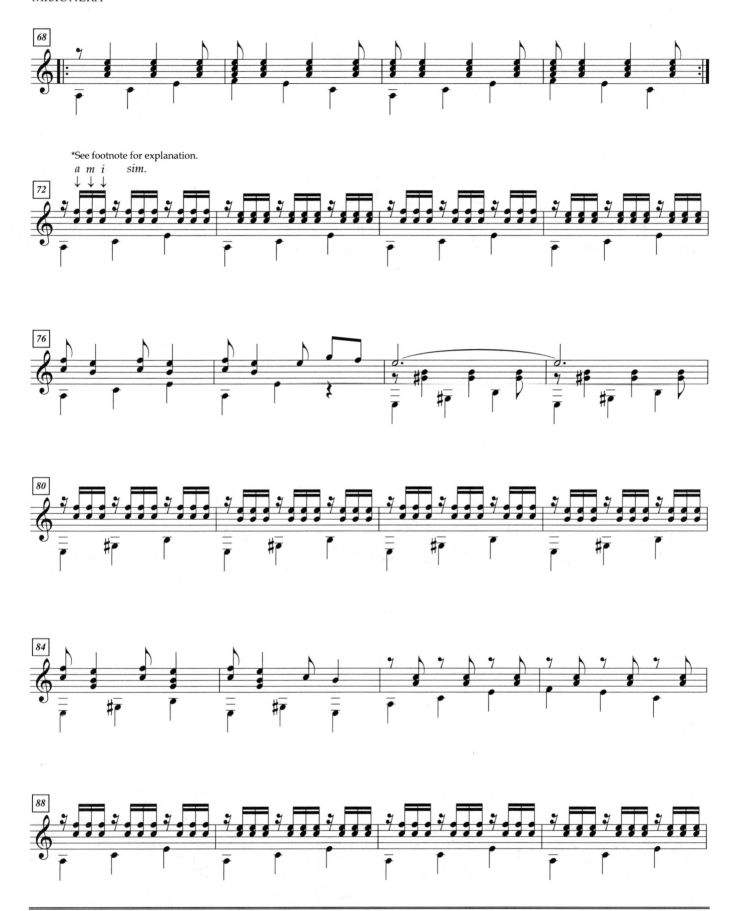

*Double tremolo. R.H. finger strokes initiate at the first string, then follow
through to the second string, resulting in a harmonization of the tremolo
effect.

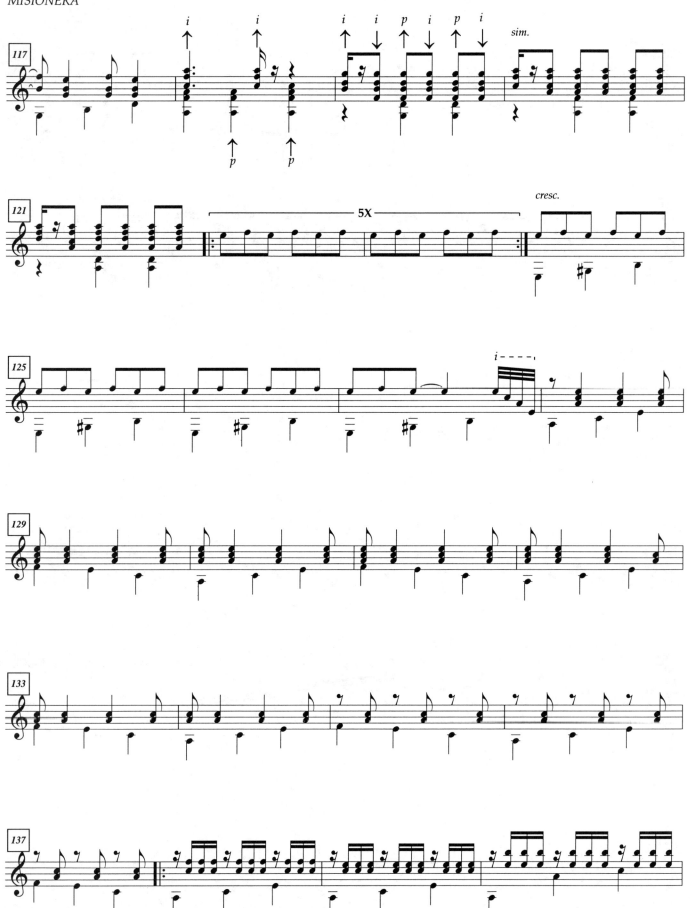

72

With daughter, Francesca and son, Jorge, in New York, 1995.

MISIONERA

from *The Artistry of Jorge Morel*
RCA LSP 3953 (1968)

FERNANDO BUSTAMANTE
arr. JORGE MOREL

Prestissimo [♩ = ca. 220]

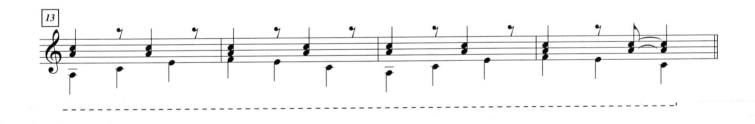

MISIONERA

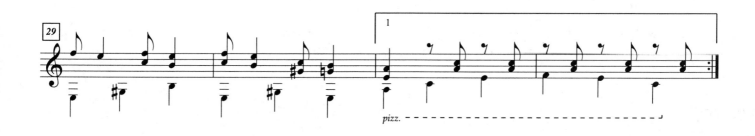

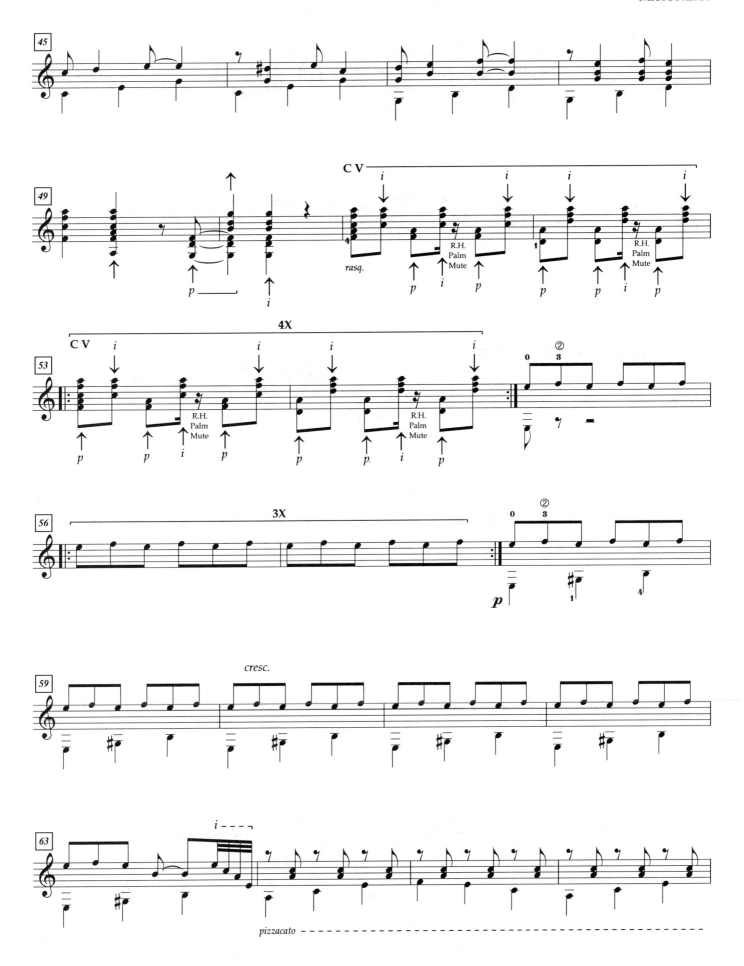

Double tremolo. R.H. finger strokes initiate at the first string, then follow
through to the second string, resulting in a harmonization of the tremolo
effect.

Jeffrey Herzlich © 2006

I See This Guy Playing My Guitar!

Here is a funny little story. Behind the stage, we had this little room to warm-up in. It was very dark; we never had good lighting in there. I left my guitar there while on break; I would go for walks. One evening, I came back and saw this guy playing my guitar! A little black guy...I didn't know who he was. He was trying to play the "Adagio" from the *Concierto de Aranjuez* by Rodrigo. I came to him and said, "Hey! Is that my guitar? Who gave you permission to play my guitar?!" He looked at me, in the dark, and I didn't recognize the man. Then Max Roach grabbed me and said, "Jorge, come! I'm sorry about this...it is Miles Davis!" [*laughs*]

Wow!

Of course, he was already very famous.

Could he play the guitar?

Yes, he could play chords. He said, "Jorge, I am sorry!" I said, "No, *I 'm* sorry!"

I sat with him and he asked me to play the *Concierto*. He recorded it, you know! He loved the piece, he was crazy about it. I remember one particular place where there is an A7 chord with a 9th in it. I played it, and he said, "Yes!!" So we went practically all the way through the entire movement together. I felt badly about over-reacting to him playing my guitar. He was a little high that night, but he was very kind to me. What a memory!

A BROADWAY STAR PLAYS THE GUITAR

Ben Vereen, the great singer, dancer, and Broadway star, stopped by my friend Tony Acosta's guitar shop about one year ago. Tony called me and said, "Jorge, Ben Vereen was here and he heard your compact disc [*Jorge Morel 1960-1980 Recordings*] playing in the store and loved it." I think the piece that Tony said was playing was "American Fantasy." He came by the store either to purchase a string or to buy a guitar. He asked Tony who was playing. Tony showed him the CD and he bought it right away! Now he knows who I am! [*laughs*]

I know Mr. Vereen plays the guitar and likes jazz. He is one of my favorite artists on Broadway, a great dancer and singer. He is still doing very well. I hope he is still playing my record.

JORGE MOREL

GUITARIST/
COMPOSER

"IMPRESSIVE
FORMIDABLE
TECHNIQUE"

"THE MOST ENJOYABLE
GUITAR RECITAL
OF THE SEASON"

NEW YORK TIMES

AT THE WIGMORE HALL

PIAZZOLLA · AYALA · MOREL · GERSHWIN · ESCOBAR

Manager: William Lyne · *Lessees:* Arts Council of Great Britain

TUESDAY 29 MAY 1990 at 7.30 pm

Presented by

CLASSICAL GUITAR MAGAZINE

Tickets: £7.00, £6.00, £5.00, £4.00

All bookable in advance from Wigmore Hall Box Office (01-935 2141) and usual agencies. Postal applications should be accompanied by a s.a.e.
Box Office Hours: Monday-Saturday, 10.00 am-8.30 pm (days without concerts 10.00 am-5.00 pm). Sundays 45 minutes prior to performance. No advance booking during half-hour prior to performance.
Telephone Bookings: Monday-Saturday, 10.00 am-6.30 pm.
Credit Card Bookings: Access, Visa, Amex, Diners. No bookings after 6.30 pm, or on Sundays, or from one hour prior to performance.
Booking Opens: To general public on 29 April and to mailing list subscribers on 22 April.

Photo courtesy of Maurice Summerfield.

A young Jorge Scibona in Buenos Aires, 1934.

My early memories are of a little guitar my parents gave me. It had wooden tuning pegs, and it sounded okay. I remember the first chord my father taught me. It was an E major chord; I practiced that chord for two weeks! [*laughs*]

I was good at sketching portraits with pencils. We used to have a school across the street from my house. It was a technical school that offered classes in art and music. I was twelve years old at this time. My mother, who was alive then (she passed away when I was very young), and my father thought it would be a good idea to enroll me in courses that could help my drawing. We went there and my father asked the director, "Do you have any classes in pencil drawing?" The director said, "No, we just offer classes in architectural drawing."

Jorge's family in Buenos Aires, 1938.
Young Jorge standing far right.

Well, this was not my thing. My father said, "No, this will not do!" So we turned to leave, and as we were walking out of the building, we heard a guitar! My father asked, "Who is playing?" The director said, "It is our guitar teacher!" My father was an amateur guitar player. He asked me, "Jorge, would you like to try it…take some guitar lessons?" Of course I thought, 'Why not?' I was young and I liked the guitar. So, my father paid for an entire year of lessons with the woman who taught guitar at this school; her name was Amparo Alvariza.

He was very confident you were going to do well!

Yes. Unfortunately, because there were not enough students enrolled in the class, it was discontinued. I guess I was showing something in the six months in that class that the other students were not. I started to like the guitar. My teacher liked me very much; she said to me, "Jorge, I will teach you!" I remember thinking, 'What am I going to do if I don't have this class?' So she started coming to my house. Now, the cost of these lessons were a lot more because these were private lessons. She asked me where I lived. I said, "Across the street!" So she came and spoke to my father concerning my lessons and my father said, "Fantastic! How much do you charge?" Now, my father could not really afford the lessons, [but he] really wanted me to study so were had two private lessons a week in my house.

You must have been making great progress since she taught you twice a week.

Yes.

You told me you were drawn to the guitar. What was the attraction?

It was the sound. I didn't have a good guitar starting out. When I first went to the school, I was playing that first guitar with the wooden pegs. My teacher looked at that little guitar and said, "It is a toy!" She told my father I needed a regular guitar and he found one for me; it was a fantastic instrument! He worked so hard to buy me that guitar.

I received that guitar about one month after the school cancelled the class. One day after school, my father said, "Go to your room!" There was this guitar. I opened the case and here was the most beautiful guitar. I kept that guitar for years and years. It was a very good Argentinean guitar. My father bought that guitar second hand from a very famous musician who had to palm it for money. My father was looking for a guitar and the guy said, "I can sell you my guitar." My father said, "But you don't have it." The guy said, "If you bring me the money, I can go get it for you." So my father brought it to me; it was one the happiest moments of my childhood and my life! Once I got that guitar, it changed my life. My approach changed and my level of interest was increased. Here was this beautiful sound; I practiced for hours and hours!

Did you know at that time the guitar would be your life?

No. I knew I liked it. I wanted to keep practicing, but I knew perhaps someday I would have to learn something else to make a living. My father didn't think that way; he was an actor.

Your father knew something about your talent that you didn't see.

He understood because he was also a guitarist. Things came out of the guitar easily for me. My teacher said, "Jorge, play Carcassi, learn this Carulli..." I said, "That's a lot of work!" I knew she would be coming again later in the week because we had two lessons a week. I didn't have much time to practice, but when she came, I had my lessons ready. She would be so happy.

After four years, my father said, "I don't think she can teach you anymore. We're going to find you a new teacher!" Then we went to Pablo Escobar. I studied with him for another five years.

Graduation day, 1949. Jorge (middle row, center)

What do you remember of the time you spent with Professor Escobar?

Pablo Escobar taught me interpretation and technique. He also taught me a little bit of composition, maybe without trying, because he was a composer and I was exposed to his music. He wrote "Chopi," and that piece has since been in my hands for many years. After the first year with him, he introduced me to the radio station where he played on a weekly show. He told me we were going to play together. He also told me to learn "Asturias" by Albéniz. He said, "You are going to play this piece on the radio next month, so learn it!" I finished with two diplomas in 1949; one for theory and the other for guitar. I have a photograph taken the day of the graduation.

Did Segovia come through during this time?

He did come, because he lived in Uruguay when he had to leave Spain because of the civil war and World War II. He came to Buenos Aires several times. I heard him in 1952 when he came to play a concert sponsored by the radio station. He played a live concert. Nobody could get tickets; only the rich 'society' people. A friend of mine at the time, a very famous soccer player said, "Jorge, do you want to hear Segovia?" I said, "Are you crazy? Of course I want to hear him!" He said, "I am going to give you a ticket and you're going in by yourself!" Because of his fame and influence, he was able to give me a ticket. We were friends from childhood; we grew up in the same neighborhood. That was the first time I heard Segovia in 1952, when he played for Radio National de Buenos Aires.

What do you remember from the concert?

"Sevilla" by Albéniz!

Was he still playing his Hauser guitar?

Yes. I was impressed by "Sevilla." I cried because of the beauty of this piece. I went to my father and said, "I want to learn to play this piece." My father said, "Jorge, you are not ready for this piece!" I worked for six months so hard, and then played it for my father. For another seven or eight months, I remember taking the guitar and changing the arrangement. Even in those days, I was changing notes to make it more musical. I did not know the piece from a guitaristic point of view. I only knew it from hearing the original piano score. I was intrigued by the timbres of the guitar, the secrets of its poetry, and of course, I wanted to do my own thing! I became very independent in my thinking and playing early on. This is just me.

After my graduation, Professor Escobar said, "Jorge, I would like to work with you some more to prepare you for your career as a classical guitarist." I thought, 'I don't want to do this, play all these pieces by the book!' So I took the reigns, came to my Professor and said, "I'm sorry, I will come by to visit as often as you want but I can't do this: continue with your offer to prepare me as a classical guitarist. I don't have the feel for it."

What was you next move?

I was doing theater. I was an actor with my father. I did this for a few years. I never took lessons. It was stage acting, mostly comedy. I did little parts. I didn't think I was a good actor, but I thought I was acceptable. My father said, "You, Jorge, you are not a bad actor but you are not a good one either!" He would get so mad at me. He put my guitar away. I cried too much and said, "Where the hell is my guitar?"

If your passion is acting...

I would have been an actor! I stayed in Argentina for a couple more years until I left for good. I actually left under contract to an acting company. They told me to bring my guitar.

So you were acting and playing the guitar every night. Did they pay you more for pulling double duty?

No! [laughs] When the contract expired, I was in Ecuador. I was in this beautiful city thinking, 'What am I going to do now?' Just then, the people at the radio station told me they wanted me to perform on the radio and they would book concerts for me. From there, I went to Colombia, and this was a rough time for me. I was hungry. I had gone a few days without food, and I am not the type of person to knock on doors begging for food. I was looking for jobs. I did not know anyone in Colombia. Finally, God was looking after me, I was playing in a club and some Argentinean friends invited me to eat with them. I started playing and this young man, a singer/guitarist came to me and said, "Jorge, what are you doing here? Where do you come from?" I said, "Buenos Aires!" He said, "Oh my God, I want to introduce you to the Ambassador for Argentina in Bogotá. He is a great guitarist!"

The Ambassador was a man from the air force. In fact, he was one of the main men from the military who fought against the dictator, [Juan] Perón. Under Perón's regime, he made a living playing the guitar in Uruguay. When he met me at the Embassy in Bogotá...oh, a beautiful place...I remember being well dressed and I played, and he went crazy! He loved me, and he asked,

"What are you doing here? When did you come?" I said,
"About two months ago."
"Do you have money?" he asked.

I told him I was staying in a hotel and they were going to kick me out because I didn't have money to pay them. I told him I did have some friends here, but they were living in the same conditions as I. This man was kind to me; he organized a big concert at the Embassy for me. He charged a lot of money from everybody to attend my concert. Many people came and he gave me everything—every bit of the money. I never had so much money in my pockets back during those days. From this opportunity, I became a regular on a television show. I played every week and by then, I was much better off; this was around 1959.

I wonder if any footage survives from those television shows.

I don't think so. While I was playing on this television show, I received a call from a man who said he saw me on the show. He owned a Spanish restaurant in the middle of Bogotá.

It was a gorgeous place! He asked me to play the exact things I played on the television show. I used to play "Misionera" there. He asked me to play two shows every night, five days a week. He offered to pay me a fair amount of money and all I can eat free! [*looks to the heavens!*] Thank you God! I was eating well…[*pauses and laughs*]…playing and eating so much! The owner came and jokingly said, "Jorge, if I knew you ate that much, I wouldn't have offered you a contract with free food!" [*laughs*] I left Colombia weighing about ten pounds heavier. [*laughs*]

From Colombia, I went to Cuba. Castro took Havana in 1960. I arrived in December of 1959 and stayed until March of 1960. A Cuban friend, whom I had helped before, arranged my stay. I also had a couple of friends from Argentina staying there too. So I began to look for jobs. When the Cubans heard my playing, I was offered the opportunity to appear again on another weekly television show and the chance to play four or five concerts. I remember meeting Juan Mercadal. He died not long ago. Of course, he was Cuban and I met him there. I never met Leo Brouwer because he was very young at this time, though I am sure he was around then.

How was Cuba at this time?

Scary! It was the beginning of Castro. Everybody was trying to make a living in Havana. I remember sitting with friends at a café in front of the United States Embassy watching people trying to get visas to get out. I learned to keep my mouth shut because it was the smart thing to do! Two months later, I left for Puerto Rico.

Puerto Rico was the bridge to the United States. It was a blessing because I met my wife there, right from the start. She was young—younger than I was. We married about six months later.

Tell me about meeting Olga for the first time.

I was staying with an Argentinean couple who were my friends. Right across the lobby of the apartment building was the apartment of Olga's sister, Ada. She had an actor friend visiting and she was, of course, friends with the couple I was staying with, so I was introduced to Ada at that time. Ada liked me immediately and introduced me to

Ada, Olga, and Jorge.

her husband. She had two sisters, Olga and Mary. She went to Olga the next day and said, "You have to meet this man!" [*laughs*] I tell everyone one, "Hey! That is the best thing Ada did in her life!" [*laughs*] Olga came the next day…eighteen years old…ah! [*kisses the air*]

She swept you off your feet!

Yes. I was older, but it did not matter. I started to talk to Olga. She loved the guitar. Every day after work, she would come to Ada's apartment to be with me. It didn't take too long. I told her, "I like you…I love you!" I knew I loved her and she knew it too! So we became engaged and then I had to make a trip to New York. When I came back, I could not wait any longer. I said, "I don't have money, but I have concerts that will make money." So she quit her job and we married…a very simple wedding. Two days later, I had to leave again for New York because I was recording *The Warm Guitar* for Decca.

That explains the phrasing and beauty in those first two albums (*The Warm Guitar of Jorge Morel* and *The Magnificent Guitar of Jorge Morel*) for Decca. You were so in love.

Yes. I was crazy in love. I said, "God helped me, because I could have ended up with someone else, or worse, I could have been just a bum." She helped me in many many ways. She was so mature. At 18 years old, she was more mature than I was. Physically and internally, she was beautiful in every way. If she did not know something, she would not open her mouth. She was a very clever girl. She read every day of her life.

As I said, we were engaged in 1961. I went to New York to make the record and to play a concert with the Kingston Trio at Carnegie Hall. It was during this time Olga finished her obligations to her employer. When I returned to Puerto Rico, we were married right away. I had to return to New York to finish the recording and to find an apartment. I found a nice little place and she came to New York in April of 1961, on Easter.

We began our life together and my life changed. I remember feeling so lonely before, all these years away from Argentina. I used to ask myself, "What am I doing with my life?" I think this girl came into my life to save me.

From what?

From what I don't know.

What did Olga bring to your life to complete you?

It was a combination of things: a great love, as I understood that girl and she understood me. We had great fun together. But I felt like I had a mother also, the mother that I did not have growing up. Not since I was 15 years old, when my mother died, did I feel the security and love I felt from Olga. She was so mature, I just felt a part of my mother in her. Could this be possible?

After the wedding, the move to New York, and the completion of the record, we went to California. New York was okay, but I was not doing a lot of work there. Olga had to go to work to make money to support us. She was a very good typist, and good at using IBM machines. Also, her English was very good. She was making more money then I was at that time.

I want to back track a little in my story, as I forgot to mention something important. The year before, in 1961—before I married Olga—I came to Carnegie Hall to play with the Kingston Trio. I played first as the opening act and they followed. We played two concerts that night to a full house—not bad for my first trip to the United States! Then, I went back to Puerto Rico because the union did not allow me to stay in New York since I was not a member or even a citizen of the United States. I married my wife and then, eventually, on the second trip, came ahead to finish the record and to look for an apartment.

After six months in New York, we traveled to California. I began an engagement at a club called The Trident, which was located near the San Fransisco Bay. It was really beautiful; you could see the Golden Gate Bridge every night. I had a ball performing there. I became friends with a great jazz pianist who played there also by the name of Vince Guaraldi, the composer of the *Peanuts* theme. He died many years ago. We played together every night in the show. He would play with a trio and I would play solo. We played for five or six months. After this, Olga and I made a short trip to Hawaii, back to California, then on to Florida, and eventually back to Puerto Rico.

I thought the return to Puerto Rico would be good for us—my daughter had not been born yet—so we decided to go. I found work playing at various clubs and hotels. It was at this time when I met Vladimir Bobri. He was a member of the Society of Classic Guitar in New York. He was president at the time of our meeting in Puerto Rico. He gave me his card and said, "Jorge, what are you doing here playing in a hotel?"

I answered, "Mr. Bobri, I have to make a living!"

"Yeah, I know. But you don't belong here! Come to New York and I will introduce to the right people. The way you play, you should be heard in the concert hall, not a hotel!"

In 1963, I played for the Society. Everybody came to my concert and the entire program, with the exception of Crespo's "Nortena," was unknown to them. The review was great and the people liked it, but they [*the society members*] didn't know how to label me. So I told them, "DON'T!"

After this concert, a woman approached me and said, "Mr. Morel, I would like to introduce you to Art D'Lugoff, the owner of the Village Gate." So next day I went to meet him and to audition. He asked me to go onto the stage and play. I remember the sound system was so beautiful. It was the best jazz spot in New York City. I sat there and played three pieces for Mr. D'Lugoff, and he said, "Okay." He did not say anything else, and I was going to ask him if he liked it or not. I decided to stay quiet, but if he did not like it, I knew I was going to be heartbroken. He finally said, "I like it!" This was not enough for me. As I left the club, he said, "I'll be in touch with you." In other words, 'Don't call me, I'll call you.' The next day he called. "Jorge, do you want to come play this weekend?" I thought, 'What?! All these legendary musicians…*me*? Play *there*?' This became a long-standing engagement for me.

Who were some of the people playing there when you performed at the Village Gate?

My first night: Bill Cosby.

How was he to work with?

He was very nice to me. He already was on his way up. I also worked with Flip Wilson; he was good to me also. Both of these men loved the guitar.

I worked at the Village Gate off and on for three years with many different people such as Stan Kenton, Erroll Garner…I played opposite to all these people!

I bet you learned a lot.

Oh, I learned so much about jazz. I came to know Herbie Mann. I played a two-week show with the Swingle Singers. I loved their Bach! Stan Kenton always drew huge crowds. One evening he introduced me. My friends told me, "Jorge, Stan Kenton introduced you tonight!" I could not believe it!

Art D'Lugoff offered to help me attain other bookings. He got an engagement for me at the Five Point Club about two weeks after I finished my engagement at the Village Gate. The Five Point Club was located in the East Village, a nice club that seated probably around 250 people. It was supposed to be a three-week job with Max Roach and his group. I played my same set of music that I played at the Village Gate and pretty much the same as play now. I was there for 14 weeks! The owner kept asking me, "Jorge, do you want to stay for another week?"

I eventually started playing more concerts. The touring took the place of staying home playing in clubs. During one of my concert tours, probably around 1967 or 1968, I played near Nashville, Tennessee. This was the first time I tried to meet Chet Atkins.

You know, Chet had already recorded several of your arrangements on his RCA album, *Class Guitar* (1967).

Yes. I remember his recording of my arrangement of Bernstein's "I Feel Pretty." During this trip to Nashville, I drove my car to a hotel there and went to the coffee shop for coffee. There was this guy there, a nice man, who asked, "Hey! Are you in show business?" I answered,
"Yes, I am." He said,
"You look like Dean Martin! Are you an actor?"
"No, I am a musician," I said. He asked what I played and I told him I played guitar.
He said, "What? You play the guitar? Do you want to meet Chet Atkins?"

I thought this guy was pulling my leg, but I took a chance. Now, I was naïve back in those days. I thought, 'What the heck! He looks like a nice man. I will go with him,' So he told me, "We are going to RCA Victor to see Chet Atkins!"

Before we went to RCA, we stopped by a beauty salon owned by his ex-wife; he wanted to introduce me to her. [*laughs*] When he came into the salon, everybody loved him. I knew I was safe, since everyone just went crazy about this guy!

So we left for RCA. As soon as he walked in the building, everybody stood up when he entered the room, it was amazing! You know the funny thing? I cannot remember his name. I could never tell Chet who this man was. Chet had an idea who he might have been, but he was never sure.

He had to be an important person for everybody to stand up when he entered the room at RCA.

Chet was not there that day. The fact that I tried to see Chet meant a lot to him. When I arrived home in New York, I mailed the album I recorded for the Spanish Music Center [*Guitar Moods, 1966*]. Chet wrote to me and said, "Jorge, this is a beautiful album...thank you so much! I am going to try to get you a record contract with RCA Victor." At this time, Chet Atkins was one of the most powerful men in the music industry.

They [RCA] called me. I recorded the album in 1968, and it was released in late 1969. The man from the agency was Charles Johns. He said, "Mr. Atkins, we would like to book you..." Chet was not interested. He was vice-president of RCA; he did not have time for this.

Chet did not say no. Instead, he took my new album and showed it to Mr. Johns and said, "This is the man you are looking for." Mr. Johns was surprised! He said, "I don't know him." Chet responded, "You will! Listen to this record. It is brand new and soon to be released by RCA. Call Jorge. He is the nicest man."

Chet gave me the most incredible recommendation. This began my relationship with Columbia Artist. Two days later, they called me and asked if I was interested in touring the United States and Canada with Community Concerts. It was a big thing for me back in those days—this was 1968! So I said, "Yes. I'll come down to the office to talk and to sign the agreement." It was a one-year agreement, which turned into six or seven years. I played hundreds of concerts under their management. All of this, because of the kindness of Chet Atkins! It was a beautiful thing he did for me.

How did you do that with such a young family?

My son, Jorge [*born from a previous relationship*] was home in Argentina with his mother. My daughter was five or six years old and my wife, Olga, stayed home caring for her while I was touring. Before Francesca was born, Olga came with me on tour all the time. Back in those times, the mother stayed home with the daughter and the father was out on the road for a month, perhaps two or three. Sometimes Olga would leave Francesca with my sister-in-law, Ada; this would allow Olga to come be with me.

Olga worried because she stopped working when Francesca was born; she really wanted to go back to work. I told her we were making plenty of money and it was not necessary for her to go back to her job. I was paid very well and I worked hard. When I would come home after a tour, we would go to the bank to deposit the money so we could pay the bills and things like that. This would sustain us until the next tour would begin two months later. In the meantime, I would do shows and teach. I was busy all the time.

With friend Roberto, brother Osvaldo, Francesca, and Olga, Buenos Aires, 1968.

What was your routine in those days?

I was playing the guitar more than I was writing music back then. Probably two or three years after that, the compositions started to grow. My desire to write was growing. I was happy playing, but I wanted to write!

Was this around 1970?

No, it was before. I had been composing since the late 1950s. I must clarify something: I consider much of the composing I did early in my career just by ear. I did not write things down. My serious composing began when I really dedicated myself to writing down every note that I wanted to hear. You see, sometimes you write by ear and you *think* you are composing something.

Do you write with the guitar in hand?

Yes, yes, always! Notating the music became a great help to me, because it allowed me to understand what I was doing much more than just kind of improvising my music.

Who are your influences or inspirations?

Very few guitarists! Most composers are not guitarists.

Probably a good thing!

I always loved George Gershwin, Claude Debussy and Maurice Ravel. I love jazz...Duke Ellington, for example. But for the guitar, it is Héitor Villa-Lobos.

He used the resources of the guitar in a very natural way.

Yes.

And of course, I presume, as you were going through the conservatory, you were exposed to the music of Agustín Barrios.

I never played the music of Barrios until I came to New York. Of course I knew of him, but never cared about him until I learned of his tremendous output of compositions. After so many years in Buenos Aires playing practically everything on the guitar, I look back and find it hard to believe I never played his music. It is even more amazing to me that my path to Barrios came when I moved to New York. I heard John Williams' old recording of Barrios and, of course, I have many old friends from South America who play his music such as Alirio Diaz, Rodrigo Riera and Carlos Barbosa-Lima. I remember hearing them play "Danza Paraguay," thinking, 'I love that piece; I want to learn it!' Barrios wrote hundreds of pieces! I wanted to learn all of them.

I think there is a wonderful parallel between you and Barrios. You both have displayed the capability to write in the classical vocabulary and, at the same time, write beautiful pieces using traditional Latin American rhythms and forms. And from a personal point of view, Barrios was known to be a man of character who showed compassion for people, just as you do.

Thank you very much! I have always tried to be humble and kind to people. I think I learned this from my father. He had a way with people; he made them happy.

In the "Sonatina" that is dedicated to David Russell, the style is much more classical; definitely a departure from my original style of composition. I have been asked many times, "Why the departure?" I can't say why. However, you still hear me in this piece. Certainly, when you hear this piece you do not say, "Who wrote this?" Not Barrios, not Villa-Lobos, not Tarrega...it is I, Jorge Morel!

When you hear two bars of Gershwin, you know it is him. I always wanted to have my own voice, but I didn't have to struggle for it. I said, "This is who I am!" If I write something that sounds like somebody else, I am not going to worry about it. I told myself a long time ago that this music is me and not somebody else's. I kept this idea in mind all the time and nothing happened. Nobody said, "Hey Jorge, are you sure that is your piece?"

When I hear your music, I hear just you.

You can hear the jazz influence mixed with Latin American rhythms: that is who I am.

In the "Millennium Duet," I hear some occasional references to Gershwin.

And Debussy! I love Debussy, and I am not ashamed of using, in just a couple of bars, beautiful dominant–ninth chords.

You know, Ravel promised a concerto to Segovia! Of course, it never happened because Ravel died in 1937, the same year as Gershwin. Ravel would have written great music for the guitar; he had some Spanish blood in him, I believe, from his mother.

It is often said that the French wrote some of the best Spanish music.

Ravel and Debussy wrote great Spanish music!

Look at some of the greatest composers of the Twentieth Century who went to Paris to study. Villa-Lobos, Ponce, Copeland, Gershwin, and Piazzolla, just to name a few.

When Gershwin went to study with Nadia Boulanger, she did not want to teach him. She said, "George, you are already a composer. You don't need me. I might ruin you!"

I heard a similar story involving Boulanger and Astor Piazzolla. She encouraged Piazzolla to be true to the tango and develop his voice within this idiom.

Yes. She was a very great lady; a great teacher.

Let us get back to you and our conversation about your touring and composing.

During the time I was touring with Columbia Artists, I did not really have time to compose or even record. I was constantly on the road: playing, playing, and playing! Practicing and playing new things. Whatever arrangement I had time to do, I did by ear. I didn't have time to put them down on paper. This took about six years of my career but eventually ended with Columbia Artists—this was around 1977 or 1978.

During those years in the 70s, I became friends with Tony Acosta. He was a soccer player, but had always played the guitar. He studied with me for a while and our friendship grew. He is a very successful man in the guitar business with his shop in Manhattan called Luthier Strings. We are like brothers!

With Ole Halen, 1987

Tony and I have done several recordings together that he produced. The newest one is the *Suite Del Sur.* [*Ed. Note: This recording is a more recent performance of Morel's concerto, which originally premiered in 1975 with the Los Angeles Philharmonic under Zubin Mehta.*] To me, this is probably my best recording because of the orchestra. I have played many concerts with chamber orchestras and symphony orchestras but have never recorded with one until now.

I went to the NAMM [*National Association of Music Merchants*] convention one year in Chicago and met Maurice Summerfield [*of Ashley Mark Publications*]. He told me he was starting a record label for guitar only and offered me a contract to come to England to record an LP. I went to England to play a tour he helped organize for me and, on another trip, I recorded my first album for Guitar Masters. That album gave me a big push because people were enjoying "Danza Brasilera." They still are. Look at David Russell's CD [Grammy Award-winning recording, *Aire Latino*]. My relationship with Maurice Summerfield has been going on for twenty years now. He has published fourteen editions of my music. We are very close friends. He is really a good man and a great businessman.

During the 1980s, through Maurice Summerfield, I toured extensively throughout England with many jazz greats such as Barney Kessel and many other fine people. Because of that first recording I made for Maurice, he was able to book many concerts in the United Kingdom for me. I remember playing in

Wigmore Hall, Queen Elizabeth Hall, and the Purcell Room. The BBC recorded me several times.

It was also during these years that I met Bill Bay in St. Louis after a concert I played for the classical guitar society. Bill met me after the concert and said, "Jorge, if you are interested, Mel Bay would be interested in publishing some of your music!" I said, "Fantastic!" I had Ashley Mark already but Bill Bay said, "Maurice and I are friends. He wouldn't mind us publishing your music." So I contacted Maurice and he was okay with the whole thing.

In 1985 began a period in my life that is very important to me. I started going to Poland on a regular basis. It was really great to look forward to that every year! The first two years I went, they didn't have any money. Once the wall came down in Berlin, the Polish people started to make more money because they were benefiting from the dollar. So we were able to go to Poland and make money. Unfortunately, these trips ended because the young man who organized the festival died. He was a great, great man and the people who took over in his place did their best but it was not the same. I did go back several times to perform with my friend, Krzysztof Pelech, who organized a couple of festivals there.

Can you share more of your thoughts of your daughter, Francesca?

I raised my daughter. I was traveling and, for a while, she was in Puerto Rico. Then, she wanted to stay in New York with friends, by herself. I was worried; she was too young for this. She always had this incredible state of mind that, 'I am going to do this and my father is going to be proud of me!'

How much is Francesca like her mother?

She is quite different. Francesca is a Taurus like me. She was born May 10th, and I on May 9th. My wife's birthday was October 23rd. My daughter's personality and temper is like mine. We have a beautiful relationship, thank God! I often think that if my daughter had not been so strong with such will power, it would have been terrible for me after the loss of her mother.

New York, 1966

Buenos Aires.

THOUGHTS ON FESTIVALS AND CONCERTOS

I think guitar festivals are very good for the guitar. No other instrument in the world has festivals such as these. You can carry your little guitar in its little box everywhere you want; unlike the cello or the bass, where a problem exists in doing this. The guitar has the capacity to play solo and with orchestra or anybody, so this is a unique instrument. In recent years, I have not toured a lot but spent most of my time concentrating on composition. I was receiving more commissions to write concertos. *Fantasia de la Danza* was written, I believe, around 1987; this piece was for chamber orchestra and guitar. Then came *Concierto Rapsodico*, but more importantly before this piece was a commission for a work without guitar. I don't know why, they just wanted me to write a piece for the Brusuela Philharmonic. The piece turned out well; they liked it, but I don't want to do that; I want the guitar to be there!

I also orchestrated the "Millennium Duet" that I wrote originally for the Hanser-McClellan Guitar Duo for orchestra only. I don't know how it sounds. I haven't had it played yet, but perhaps it will be done for some future concert in St. Louis with the orchestra. Maybe the Hanser-McClellan duo would play the original duo version followed by the orchestral version; I think that would be great!

Pepe Romero, Jorge, and Celin Romero at the GFA, 1997.
La Jolla, California.

David and I met in 1979 in England. I stayed with him a for a couple of days, and he went through my music and found the "Sonatina" manuscript. He sight-read the piece and was taken by it. He said, "I like it! I want to play it!" So, I put his name on the dedication right away. He played it all over the world for many years. Finally, he recorded it, and look what happened! This CD with the "Sonatina," along with some of my other pieces, won a Grammy. This honor not only helps David and me, but most importantly the guitar—the classical guitar—or whatever you want to call it. It helps our profession and brings attention to the guitar.

With David Russell at West Dean College, England, 1991.

FIVE ENCORES AND FIVE BOTTLES OF WINE

On May 9, 1986, a concert celebrating my birthday was held in Krakow, Poland. Jorge Cardoso and Eduardo Falu bought many bottles of wine for that evening. The people in the audience sung "Happy Birthday," in Polish. This was really something; I almost cried. It was so beautiful, nearly 500 people singing to me. After I walked off the stage, Jorge and Eduardo gave me a bottle of wine. They had a bottle of wine for each encore I played that evening. [*laughs*] I never play more than two encores. Because it was my birthday, I played five encores and we had a nice celebration with five bottles of wine!

With Jorge Cardoso in Krakow, Poland, 1986.
Another encore, another bottle! Happy birthday, Jorge!

Jamming with George Benson.

"*Jorge Morel is one of the greatest guitarists/composers of all time. His broad range of musical interests stretches boundaries and makes him unique in the world of guitar.*

His early recordings were among the first that captured my imagination forty years ago and set me on my own musical journey. His West Side Story *and Gershwin medleys are classics, and his composition, "Sonatina," is one of my favorites. I will forever be grateful!*" —Earl Klugh

With Joe Pass in Finland, 1988.

THE JAZZ MASTERS SEEM TO LIKE ME MORE...

I love Gene Bertoncini. He feels the music like no other jazz guitarist I know. He is special; his touch is so unique. He is a master arranger for solo guitar.

Barney Kessel and I toured England and Ireland together. He emceed our concerts. He was as great a comedian as a guitarist. He made us laugh, and his humor made life easier during our difficult touring schedule. I remember meeting Jim Hall in Finland, and touring also with Joe Pass in Italy. This tour came not long before he passed away. He was a beautiful man and artist. They all told me, "Jorge, what you do, your playing sounds improvised!" I said, "It is not; I have to write it down!"

They appreciated me, these great men of jazz. I admired them so much and I was genuinely touched by the knowledge that they liked my music. Jazz is important in my arranging and composing. Having these experiences with them really enriched me; they were so creative when they played. I heard them every night and it was never the same, it was fresh! This caused my desire to arrange music that sounds like that. I am a 'jazzer' at heart!

With Gene Bertoncini, 2004.

"Jorge has always been one of the most inventive performer/composers in the guitar world. He brings his warm, uplifting melodic and harmonic spirit to every one of his compositions, transcriptions and arrangements, and has greatly expanded the guitar repertoire for all.

He is also a very giving and supportive person, quick to help and encourage all of us trying to learn his beautiful instrument. Thank you, Jorge." —Gene Bertoncini

Guitarreando

"Guitarreando" or "Run Away Guitar" as the Decca record executives called it on my record, *The Magnificent Guitar of Jorge Morel,* was born in Cuba in 1959. The literal translation of the title is "playing the guitar."

RUN AWAY GUITAR
"GUITARREANDO"
from *The Magnificent Guitar of Jorge Morel*
Decca DL 4966 (1963)

JORGE MOREL

*Together at the mixing desk while recording **The Warm Guitar** for Decca, 1961.*

HE SENT ME OLGA

When I met her in Puerto Rico, I was a young man and drinking maybe a little too heavy at times. I felt like I needed someone to stop me. 'Who is this person? God, please help me.' And that's what happened: He sent me Olga. So beautiful and so intelligent. So clever. And younger—eleven years younger than me. We met, and we just started to joke about getting together, because she was so young. She was eighteen or nineteen.

She said, "Jorge, I'm doing this, this, and this…" This was in Puerto Rico, and you know how they dress in Puerto Rico: wow! I went *crazy*. I was not going out with other girls, but when I met Olga, and I saw these other girls, I thought, 'Nobody can top this girl.' I didn't care for anybody else. So we started going out, and she paid for dinner because I didn't have any money. She was working, and she was making more money than I was. Then, I went to New York to record *The Warm Guitar*. I have one picture from that first evening, or maybe the next evening, where she was with me at the mixing board.

Jorge's father telling a joke. Buenos Aires, 1963.

MY FATHER

My father was a great actor in the fifties and sixties; a radio and theater actor. He was also an amateur guitarist; that is why I play the guitar. But then, at one point, he said, "Jorge, you can be an actor. Do you want to come with us, with the company?" I asked,

"Do you want to pay me?" He said,

"No." I said,

"Well, why not?" He said,

"Well, first, I want to know how good you are. Then, maybe I can hire you."

I then said, "Well Daddy, I will go with you anyway." So I went. Then he said,

"Jorge, you are not a bad actor, but you're not a good one, either. You are a good musician. As a musician, you are *far* better. Stick with the guitar." So, that's what I did.

He was great guy. Jesus Christ! My father was a man that, if he was here tonight, we would all be laughing and laughing. He lived his life—almost eighty years—to make people laugh with jokes and good will. This was his life. He was an actor, and comedian. He woke up in the morning and did what he had to do. He lived alone, because he lost my mother very early, and then he lost his second wife also. He said, "I'm very happy alone. I don't want anybody."

One morning, a long time ago, I was staying with my brother in Buenos Aires in an apartment about a half-hour from him. He didn't drive, so he took a bus to come over, and rang the bell. He said,

"Open the door! What are you doing?!" We said,

"We're sleeping! It's 8:30 in the morning! What do you want?!"

"I want to come upstairs!"

"Okay." We opened the door. He came upstairs. He said,

"I want to tell you a joke, and then I'll leave." This was an unusual father. My brother and I, tired, are both back in bed. "Daddy, what's the joke? Tell us."

"Look, there's a lion, and Indian…" whatever the joke was. His jokes were quick, because those were the funniest ones. When he finished, my brother and I were lying on floor laughing, because it was really funny. I said, "How could you do this to us? Wow!" We couldn't sleep anymore. Then he said, "Okay. I'll meet you at about one o'clock for lunch at so and so's place. That's it!" And he left, happy…a happy man, as long as you listened to his joke, had lunch with him—at *least* lunch and, if possible, dinner too—then he was the happiest man in the world. After he ate with you and told you a couple of jokes, he didn't care anymore; you could go anywhere you want. He'd say, "I'm going home." That was his life.

My father was a character that made at least one generation in Argentina laugh for years and years. They all loved him. And he was never hanging around old people. He hated old people, because he was already old. He'd say, "I can't hang around these people; they're old! They make me sick!" All of my father's friends were at least twenty, maybe thirty years younger than he was. These people wanted him in the cafes. They called him 'Mingo,' because his name was Domingo. In English, the Española name 'Domingo' means 'Sunday.' Domingo Scibona: a great actor, a great character, and a great friend. Also, the man who bought me my first guitar.

Yes, that guitar was incredible. It was waiting in my room. My father said, "Hey, go to your room. You'll find something there. Open it up!" And I see the gorgeous instrument, from 1928. This was in 1940. It had a *pure* sound. I picked up that guitar and said, "Daddy, I can't believe this." I cried. I kept that guitar forever. Later in my life, I went to Cuba and took it to a guitar maker there; because the guitar was beat up so much. The maker said he would fix it, but do you know what he did? He changed the top, completely. You take the heart, and that's it. What's left? That's what he did to my guitar. I almost cried. I said, "What did you do?!"

The guitar was not the same anymore. My father cried when I told him that. I said, "Well, I didn't know what to do. I traveled with that guitar so much and played." I went so many places with that guitar, for years. Even in my old neighborhood, my friends would call me because I was the guy that could entertain a little bit. They'd say, "Play this. Play that." And then, singers; I would accompany them. Tango singers, mainly. You know, at four o'clock in the morning. Sambas, chaquarerras, milongas.

There would be a party, a barbeque. "Jorge, come!" I *knew* that I had to bring a guitar. So I did, automatically. And my father was a proud man, because everywhere we went, he would say, "I am going to bring my son, and you'd better listen to him." From the moment I started playing, if something like this was heard [*the sound of silverware being moved*], he would stop me. "Hey, c'mon! Either you listen, or you don't!" He was so incredible. I would say,
  "Daddy, Daddy, that's okay." He'd say,
  "No! It's not okay! Shut up!" He made everybody shut up. He was so incredible! His own family—his sister—stopped talking to him because of this. He said, "I don't give a damn." Not 'damn'…he said something else. "If they want you to play, they're going to listen to you." He took me all over the place. I was thirteen, fourteen, fifteen years old—a little boy. My dad would say, "Come here. Play." I was playing things like the *Variation of Mozart* by Fernando Sor, you know? "Asturias." He was protecting me, really. He took me to the radio. Because he was an actor, he knew a lot of people in the acting field. "He's not an actor, but listen to him." And whoever made a little noise would make him so upset, so *mad*.
  "Hey! When you listen to Segovia, would you talk?!" And they would say,
  "No."
  "So, why are you talking now?!" An incredible personality.

When he died, I was there. My brother called me and said, "Jorge, come. Dad is not well, and you should come because this may be the last time." And it was. I was with him in the hospital and he told me stories. The nurses told me, "Your father is incredible." Up until the day he died, he made people laugh. Then, he died.

He was telling jokes to the doctors and nurses, and then he passed away. That was his life. I think that we all have one commitment in life; that we come here for something. I really believe that. We all have something to do here, if you know what it is that you are here for. I didn't know; I just played the guitar—tried to be a good person, a good friend. I think I was a good father. I think I *am* a good father, and I think I was a good husband…and a good son. Oh God! I'm talking too much about me!

Jorge with Francesca in Orlando, Florida, December 2002.

Sailing to London: Jorge and family aboard the Queen Elizabeth II, 1971.

Whenever I tell this story, I suffer so much. That was a very terrible time in my life: I was forty-two, losing my wife at thirty-one years old—with a baby ready to be born—and they both died.

It was a massive blood clot to the lungs, an embolism. She collapsed while cooking one evening. Just as she was starting to cook, she fell down…couldn't breathe anymore. Her belly was almost at nine months. The baby was due in June, and this was May 16, 1973. My daughter was running around the house with two friends that just came from Argentina. My wife was cooking there for *us*, with this big belly. She just fell. My daughter came running to me and said, "Daddy! Daddy! Mommy fell down. Mommy's lying down. What happened? With the fork in her hand." I thought, 'Jesus Christ!' My friend came, an Argentinean lady, and she started to give Olga mouth-to-mouth resuscitation. But Olga wouldn't come up. Nobody could save her, because there was blood coming from her legs to the lungs. If it came to her brain, she would probably have survived and become a vegetable for the rest of her life. But this went to the lungs, so she couldn't breathe. When you see that, and you're *not able to help*, you go crazy and say, "God! What can I do?!" What? I kissed her, and I grabbed her.

I went outside running from the apartment building, crying and screaming. Two cops came to the building with a car there for something else; I don't know what the hell they were doing there. They saw me so desperate, at six o'clock in the afternoon, and they said, "What happened?!"

I said, "My wife! My wife!"

They said, "Where?"

I said, "Here, [*apartment*] 1A!" So, they came with me. We grabbed my wife and took her to the car. She was *heavy*, because she was eight and a half months pregnant. I sat in the back seat with her, and the two cops sat in the front, driving us to the hospital, which was about five blocks from the apartment. Six o'clock in the afternoon in New York on Queens Boulevard was incredible because of the rush hour. So they went to the curb, and didn't respect any lights. And I am sitting with my wife. I touch her, and I see no life. Everything was cold: her head, her face. I grabbed her hand…cold. She was dead right there—she was dead *before* that. I didn't want to believe that; I thought it was a dream. I thought, 'Thirty-one years old. Pregnant. She's giving me this other child. And she's gone? Just like that?'

At the hospital once they had admitted her, I waited there for about ten or fifteen minutes; it felt like hours. They came out and said, "Mr. Morel, we did what we could." I thought they were talking about the *baby*. I thought, 'Well, they couldn't save the baby, but they saved my wife.' No. They didn't save anybody. My wife and her unborn baby were gone. So I went inside, and they asked me if I wanted to see her, and I said yes.

My daughter lives in Orlando now; she is there with her two cousins. She is doing well, but I miss her so much. I go there very often. She was eight when her mother passed away. When I came back from the hospital, she thought I was coming back with her mother and the baby. That was the idea; my wife was having a baby. But I came back all by myself, crying like crazy. I grabbed my daughter; hugged and kissed her, and she said, "Daddy, please, don't cry… you have me."

She told me, "Don't cry, because what happened to Mommy happens to *so many*. We are okay." She was trying to consol me, because I was *crying*. And believe me, I couldn't stop. I felt bad, because I thought, 'She's eight years old. She can't take this from her own father; she shouldn't have to.' But, she was stronger than me. She's now thirty-nine, and she's a great lady; so much willpower. And brilliant, really, believe me. When I go to Orlando to visit, we talk about my wife. "Remember Mom? Remember this? Remember that…" There are pictures all over her place. My nieces that grew up with my wife are all in Orlando also. We always look at pictures and watch old home movies. There's always a lot of stories to tell.

My daughter helped me to keep going; my music, and my friends also did. It's hard. You are committed to something, and I loved this lady so much—why was she taken from me? Can I just say that I don't believe in God anymore? No. I do believe in God—even more than before. She just…had to go. That's all.

She told me many times, "You know Jorge, I have a feeling that I'm not going to live too long."

I'd say, "Come on, Olga. Jesus Christ! Don't say these things. You know I don't like this." Because she went to one of those crazy palm readers.

"They told me I'm not going to live that long."

I said, "Who cares?! You *believe* in these things?"

But unfortunately, that is what happened. Maybe she had that in mind. Is that really possible? That a person can believe she will die at a given time? I don't know. She wanted to live, of course. You see, before she died, she had this spell. I called the doctor, and he said, "Please, come to me tomorrow." *Her* doctor, the one that was taking care of the baby. And the next day, she felt so good that she said, "No. Maybe that was just something [strange] that happened. I'm going to keep the appointment for next week." So she called the doctor and said, "I'm okay, I'm coming next week, Monday or Tuesday." And then, Wednesday, May 16th, 1973, when we came back from the airport, that was it.

With daughter Francesca in New York, 1972.

OLGA
I. Cancion

JORGE MOREL

OLGA
I. Cancion

OLGA
I. Cancion

II. Fughetta

123

III. Giga

OLGA
III. Giga

OLGA
III. Giga

Photo courtesy of Jim McLaughlin © 2005

I am a religious person, but I am not a fanatic. I don't go to church but there is one next door to where I live. I go there when I want to be alone. I love the ambience. I sit there wishing I had my guitar.

I worship God and Jesus Christ all the time. I read my Bible and I thank God not only because I am alive after what I have been through—the tragedies of my past. I thank God for my good health, knock on wood! I read the Bible, learn things all the time, and thank God for my life, for my daughter, and my friends.

God gave me this gift, to pick up the guitar at 75 years of age and still play. I have been doing this for a long time. When I was 25 years old, I was already into this religious belief. I do believe more and more every day. I often ask why I received the gift of music and the person next door did not?

I feel sorry for people who don't believe in God. I have friends who don't believe. I love them and they love me. They believe in something. I do believe God sent Jesus to save the world. People ask, "Why did this or that happen if there is a God?" If you are going to stop believing because of the tsunami, what are you going to do? You will be open to tragedy all the time. You will have no excuses.

Without faith or belief, what is the point of living?

There are certain things that are meant to be and we don't know what will happen to us. So you must go about being a good person trying to help.

You don't go around saying, "God doesn't give a damn about people who suffer in the world." Or, "Why did Hitler kill millions of innocent people?" Is it God's fault? If you are going to blame God for that, you are going to be in trouble with other things.

I often ask this of my friends who don't believe in God. I say to them, "Many good things happen in the world every day that we don't hear about." We only hear about the bad things, because the media makes money on people's pain. When something good happens, they don't care. Good happens every day, every minute!

We try to put God into a box, and then try to make Him like us. By doing this, we try to rationalize his wishes for us based upon our narrow understanding.

Nobody knows God's purposes for us. We should just behave well in life! We all came into this world for something. People are happy to do a simple task with their life, and they are not Chopin, they are just everyday people. They are content.

Someone who works hard and raises his or her family has just as much merit as an artist, composer, or the President of the United States.

Listen, I don't want to wear his pants! [*laughs*] No way! For all the millions of dollars, he can have it. He is doing his best; I hope he succeeds. I think this country is going to succeed, because face it: this is the greatest country in the world! *But,* if you don't handle it well, eventually it is not going to be the greatest. I don't want to move, this is my home. I want to die here because I care about this country.

I love my daughter and because of the dangers in world today—the Iraq war—we should not be there in the first place. Oh…we have changed subjects to politics!

Father and daughter, 1993.

My dad is my best friend! My mom died when I was eight years old. After that, I went to Puerto Rico for about three years to be with my grandmother. During this time, I grew up with my cousins. My dad finally became settled. He was a little nuts after everything that happened. He brought me back to New York, where he had to deal with me on his own at that time. I look back now as an adult, he being a single parent—a single man—dealing with daughter who was going through the whole teenage thing; that was rough! He did a good job. I am not boasting. I know him and I know myself, and I could have gone either way. I could have been into drugs and this and that, but he trusted me. This is a man who traveled, always on tour and he trusted me to use good judgment.

When I was eighteen years old, he would leave for a week on tour and say, "The neighbor is going to check on you from time to time to make sure you are okay!" I remember having friends over, and by eleven p.m., telling them they had to leave and go home, just as though he was there. My moral standards came from him because of our close relationship.

New York, 1967.

I believe you realized the amount of suffering you both went through and did not want to cause him any more distress. You grew up quickly.

I never wanted to disappoint him. I matured faster than most people because of what we went through.

Your dad told me of your compassion and strength shown to him the day of your mother's passing. What do you remember?

I remember everything. We had company; my grandfather had been with us the entire weekend. That same day, we drove him to the airport and then another couple from Argentina came out to stay with us. They were all hanging out in my bedroom. I remember my mom always had long hair! That week, she cut it really short…just cut it off!

I remember coming down the hall, running into the kitchen, and I saw her frying chicken. I remember chicken. The next time I walked around, I saw her at the table holding her head. She said, "Get your dad!" Then all hell broke loose. I am being dragged into the neighbor's house. The last image I have of my mom was her lying on a stretcher. I remember Dad walking back in later; he was hysterical. I ran into the bathroom and threw up! I knew what happened. I was young, but I understood.

The next memory of being on an airplane flying back with my grandfather to Puerto Rico. He had returned and now we were flying back. From that point, I was living in Puerto Rico for the next 3 years. They buried my mom there. I did not go to the funeral. They wanted me to remember her as she was in my mind: alive.

I have cassette tapes that my dad made from a reel–to–reel recorder of us. I played these tapes for my cousin the other day—my Mom must have been getting on to me for something. You hear her voice. My cousin said, "Who are *you* yelling at?"

She thought it was you and not your mom!

That was my mom! She was yelling at me; it was really funny. To hear her voice brings me back. I think I was only three years old. You can always tell on those tapes I was daddy's little girl. If my mom said, "No!", you can hear me running to my dad. It is funny how that started so early on in our relationship.

Tell me something about your dad that people don't know.

The one thing I know Dad probably never talks about—my aunt Ada would be the first one to tell you: my dad is the clumsiest man you will ever meet! We will be somewhere, and my whole family used to say, "Watch out for the wine glass. Move it or it will spill." It is only because he would just turn and hit it with his elbow. He will not see it. Even now, I feel like I am his mother. I am constantly watching after him. I am not sure if it is clumsiness or absent-mindedness.

Aunt Ada and I were just talking about the time when my mom, dad, and I were to going to Puerto Rico to visit my aunt. She had just gotten a new puppy. We told my dad, "Be careful, we know how you walk. Don't step on the puppy when you go the bathroom." No sooner had we told him this…all you heard was the dog screaming and my dad cursing! [*laughs*] If you talk to any member of my family, they will tell you this story. We always laugh about it.

Every year on my mom's birthday, my mom would tell my dad, "Listen Jorge, don't buy me that cake!" My mom hated this particular cake, and every year he would surprise her by buying it. My aunt Ada saw this, because she lived with them for a while. My mom would look at her as if to say, "Here we go again." [*laughs*]

The funny thing is he accidentally purchased the same cake every year.

Same one, same cake. My aunt and my mom were very close, and one day my aunt was telling me about how they would wake up in the morning and start cooking breakfast together. My dad wakes up and thinks he wants to cook breakfast. If my aunt tells you this story, you will be in tears because it is so funny! She starts telling you, "You know, your dad is sitting there thinking he is the greatest chef in the world—like the cook on television, flipping pancakes with the frying pan, trying to impress the girls." All of a sudden, as we were sitting there, he flips the pancake and it becomes stuck on the ceiling. I don't know what he put in the pancakes but when the pancake fell, it rolled out of the kitchen like a quarter!" [*laughs*] I said to her, "Are you kidding me?" She said, "No, it rolled across the floor, out of the kitchen!" These are stories I know he

will not tell you, but these are the ongoing human tales of my dad. These are the stories that we as a family tell that are endearing.

This story is classic. I remember being in the car for this one. I was young. When he was with RCA, he had a tour that took him into some rural places in Ohio. No city: definitely country.

The boondocks!

Yes. We were going to some airport, or trying to get out of an airport. We were trying to go somewhere, and the next thing we know, my dad starts freaking out. Somehow he made a wrong turn and we are on the runway! [*laughs*] An airplane is taking off, my dad does a 360, and halls ass out of there! [*laughs*] How he got onto the runway is beyond me. This is the stuff that goes on and on with us. Next time you talk to him, ask him about this. Leave it to my dad to get himself into something like that—on a runway of an airport.

In all fairness to him, he was probably deep in musical thought!

Even now I laugh. I am 41 years old. He comes here, and I feel like his mother now. He still treats me like his 12–year–old little girl. He calls me every single day—at least twice a day. If he doesn't call me, I get ticked off! I said to him, "You call every day, so don't all of a sudden stop calling!" I really appreciate his concern for me, because it gives me peace of mind by talking to him. This way, I know he is okay.

Even when I lived in New York, I might only see him once a week, but he would call me every day. My dad loves to come to Orlando to visit but he would be bored living here. All his friends are in New York. On Saturday nights they all hangout at Dad's. They eat, drink wine, have jam sessions with all these guitars. I'd rather go to New York to see him than have him die of boredom down here, away from his friends.

The reason I talk so loudly is that I had to talk on top of the guitar growing up! [laughs] Dad would be practicing and Mom would be cooking. It was a nice, calm environment. Even to this day, I cannot be in my house unless I have music playing. I can't function without music.

I can remember when I was 6 years old, hearing Dave Brubeck's music being played in my house. Every time I go visit my dad, while he cooks for me, I want to hear "Take Five." After dinner, growing up, my mom, dad and I would walk down Queens Boulevard, which was just outside the door. We would go to Baskin Robbins for ice cream and walk back home.

Simple pleasures!

Yes. I remember Flip Wilson being a huge part of our family. Though my parents made me go to bed at a reasonable time when I was little, I remember laughing with my parents at Flip Wilson. I loved 'Geraldine.' The laughter has stayed with me all these years. When I see the old reruns, it all comes back to me.

Your dad worked with Flip Wilson and Bill Cosby at the Village Gate.

I kept all the old posters. My mom had started a scrapbook of my dad. I tried to take over but it was so overwhelming. You see he worked with Bill Cosby and all the big names. I remember bumping into Bill Cosby—all these people were surrounding him—and all I wanted to say was, "I am Jorge Morel's daughter!" You never forget where you started. You forget all the stuff in between but not the beginning. Bill Cosby would remember my dad and mom. I have an old album signed from him to my mom.

My friends love my dad. When he visits me in Florida, they ask, "When are you going to invite us over for dinner?" They don't give a crap about seeing me; they want to be with my dad. He is so funny. He is real. My friends feed off of that vibe from him.

Tell me about eBay.

I was so upset! I spent about a month looking for old memorabilia. I went onto eBay and found a new, unopened copy of my dad's RCA album [*The Artistry of Jorge Morel, 1968*]. It was the one where he is wearing a blue turtleneck shirt. I love that album. Because it was sealed, and brand new, I thought, 'Oh my gosh! I have to have this! Nobody is going to bid on this; it is mine!' So I bid, like, fifty cents, and then a bid comes in for three dollars. I remember thinking, 'Hey, I am his daughter!' So the bidding war continues for about a week until I won the bidding at fifty-five dollars. I was so excited because I won! I didn't tell my dad, I wrapped it up and put it under the Christmas tree. Because it was sealed, I thought it would have more meaning to him.

He opens it up; he can not believe I found this record. I have pictures of him holding the record after he tore off the wrapping paper. Then, my cousin, who is like my big sister, said to him, "Theo, I don't have any of your records." So he rips the plastic off and signs it over to her! [laughs] I was hyperventilating! I said, "You don't know what I went through to get this album!" To this day, I throw this story in his face. I really don't care that he gave the record away; it was for my cousin. I just like to tease him.

It doesn't surprise me that he would do that; he is humble.

He does not realize how people talk about him. I know what he is about. I know how people react around him, something as simple as my friends from school. Going back to when I was in high school, when my dad would play a concert in New York, I wanted certain close friends of mine to come with me to his concert, because he was my dad. My friends did not understand his level, they just knew him as the man who was always playing guitar in the kitchen, or cooking something, or yelling at me for whatever.

I remember taking three of my good friends to his concert at Alice Tully Hall. We all got 'decked out.' One of these friends who stands out in my memory said, "Oh my God! I see this man doing laundry everyday, going to the grocery store, carrying his shopping bags. I can't believe this is the same man I deal with everyday!"

My dad is just a regular guy! Here is another good story.

This is really funny! I was not involved in it, but it is hysterical! My ex–husband, Nick, was a big heavy metal fan. All his friends were metal guitarists.

These guys had to know who your dad was.

That is what is so funny, because my ex-husband didn't: he was the singer. One day while we were dating—Nick takes pictures of everything—he wanted Dad to sign over all these 8X10 pictures. He had these albums because he used to work for *Billboard* magazine. Nick and his friends came over one weekend and started rummaging through Dad's old albums. I was laughing because these metal dudes stopped and said, "When did you meet this guy?" Nick said, "What?" His friends said, "You know him? You met him?" Nick said, "Man, that is my girl's dad!" It was so funny because he was freaking out over learning who my dad was. So Nick's friends *had* to come over to meet my dad somehow. My dad didn't care; he was just having fun!

I think Dad had a concert in Chicago, so Nick decided he was going with him to be his 'roadie.' Nick's best friend, Fabio, who is a great guitarist, said, "I am going with you!" I was there, and this was my husband at the time and his best friend—two long haired metal guys—going with my dad to a classical concert. Nick cracked me up. He said, "You had to see all these women losing their minds! It was like a rock concert!" After the concert, all these women starting talking to Nick and Fabio: they were trying to get to my dad. Nick said, "Look at all these older ladies coming on to me. They don't want me, they want him!" That evening was a revelation to Nick and Fabio.

My dad has remained real. He has a good heart…sometimes too good. I get annoyed, because I feel sometimes he is naïve. This is my dad's genuine nature and he will not change.

I know where you are going with this: people take advantage of his kindness.

Yes, exactly!

I love all my dad's old recordings. There are some pieces that he used to play that he never recorded. I know there are things that he cannot play the way he played them back when I was growing up. I could sing these tunes to you if I had a voice. I remember every note. My favorite was "Holiday for Strings." It was his great arrangement, the most kick-ass version, seriously! To this day, I don't think anybody could play it the way he played it. I told Dad the other day he should go back and play it the way he used to. Of course, I said, "You need to do it fast, like the Bionic Man!" I remember how he played it when I was growing up. Though it is meant for piano, he made this unbelievable arrangement for guitar. It is vivid in my memory how he played it. Now, when he plays it, it is much slower. I want to hear it 'go!' It is an out of this world arrangement!

There is one person in my dad's life to me who is family. He is a guardian angel for my dad: it is Tony [Acosta]. He has been that perfect uncle. When I was growing up—when my dad would be worried about me—Tony would tell him not to worry and to trust my judgment. Tony has always been a great supporter of Dad and me.

Let me tell you something about my dad. If you have ever been around him when he is practicing at home…I have to laugh! When I was younger, I remember asking, "What is he yelling at?" He would be practicing. When I was in high school, getting dressed in the morning—I was so in tune with his playing—if he played a wrong note, I would hear it immediately. I love going to his concerts, but I become so stressed out. If he makes a mistake, he will improvise something to cover and nobody hears the original flaw. He will make up something completely spontaneous and then, bam! Back to the original tune. I know his playing and when he does this, I become a nervous wreck.

I always tell your dad, "I hear your love for Olga in those early Decca records. There is something very emotional in your phrasing."

There is so much love in those records. I know what you mean. It is probably bad that I do this: every relationship I have been in is patterned after my parents. I don't mean the typical married thing. I never saw them fight; I know they did—all couples do—but not in front of me. All I saw was my dad pinching my mom's butt! [*laughs*]

That old dog!

I saw the fun, the laughter: that is what I remember. That is what I am looking for in a relationship: the fun and romance they lived. That is what I grew up with. Kids grow up in families where the husband is beating the wife and the kids, and the kids grow up thinking this is okay. I was brought up in a family that was always very happy, loving, and fun. My mom always said to Dad "Jorge, stop!" He would pinch her ass, grab her, and kiss her. That is what I remember. That is what I am looking for in a relationship—what my parents had: love.

Krakow, Poland, 1986.

"Jorge Morel has been my friend and musical brother for 35 years.

A more wonderful gentlemen you'll never meet. Before my wife passed away, we both loved Jorge because of his kindness, his sweetness, and his generosity of spirit. He is the best not just as a musician, but as a human being. He is my friend.

Music is his love,

Composition is his gift,

Playing is his joy, and the guitar is his mistress!

He is indeed 'EL MAESTRO'"
—Jean-Jacques Delaveau

You are Something Extraordinary!

August 10, 1979

Dear Jorge Morel,

It was my pleasure to hear and meet you at last, after so many years of knowing you only as a respected name. Your name is not yet known here, except among the most well informed of aficionados—and, after hearing you in concert, I must say it is a pity. A pity too that so few people came; this, I think, was the product of:

1. Inept publicity verging on the non–existent.

2. The almost totally unfamiliar nature of your program. Now I am among the sternest critics of what we call 'rent-a-programme' but I realize that SOME familiar content is necessary to lure the cautious. Also, so many items were of what many would call 'light' character that it gave a false impression of your quality. I was not the only one to be told that someone was not going because you were "probably a sort of coffee-bar or cabaret guitarist!" Had your so-called agent been astute enough, he would have approached the musical journals in advance, making it clear that you are something extraordinary.

Your concert made one of the strongest impressions of any I have heard in a long time. You are a true artist, and there should have been many more people there to receive that message.

My very best wishes, and thanks for a splendid evening.

Sincerely,

John Duarte
London, England

The Guitar Masters recordings were my first recordings in the 1970s. The first album was recorded in the United Kingdom in 1979. I was silent for nearly a decade. I still do not understand why, as in that decade I played more concerts than I ever have played in my entire career. Nobody wanted to record me, until Maurice Summerfield ask me to come to England to make that first record. I remember using a Kohno Model 30 on the first album for him. I played a beautiful Manuel Rodriguez on the second album and on the last album, I played a guitar by Robert Ruck which I purchased from Eliot Fisk.

If you compare my RCA record from 1968 to my Guitar Masters recordings of the late 1970s and early 1980s, the mood is different. The tragedy changed my life. It made me more aware of my purpose for being here, and for how long. Why do this or that, if something such as what happened might occur again in my life? I believe we should make each moment, each day, count, and I think you can hear this on those recordings.

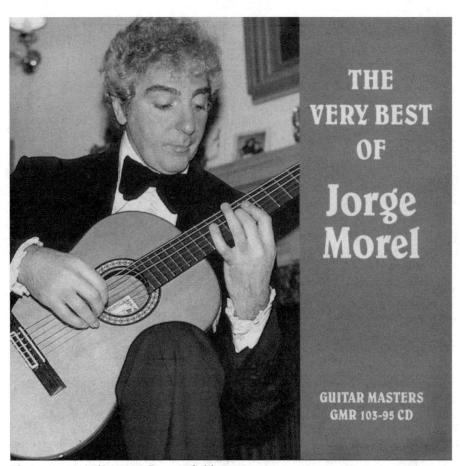

Photo courtesy of Maurice Summerfield.

*"I believe we should make each
moment, each day, count..."*

I think classical guitarists today try to be more diverse and broader in the use of popular forms, jazz, and the music of South America. Latin American music, well written and arranged for the guitar, is very important for the instrument. I feel very happy to be a part of this movement.

Latin American guitar literature has been successful for many years, now even more than ever. When we say Latin America, before we spoke of only a few countries, not all of them. When you say Latin America, many people think of *salsa* from Cuba, which is beautiful. But Argentina, Brazil, Venezuela, Columbia, Ecuador—places I have been to—I have listened to their music and I love it! In each country, people would ask me to play music from their country. For example, in Puerto Rico, they would ask for "Lamento Borincano." I always tried to please my audience. I learned many years ago to arrange music to please the people, and they liked it very much. When I came to America, it was a different story.

I dedicated more time to the traditional repertory when I came to the United States. I wanted to play Albéniz and I transcribed the pieces myself. I did this because I was not taken seriously by the guitar world. When I went to England, they really appreciated me. In those past years, I wanted to show everyone that I could do everything. I remember once in England being asked to play something during one of my master classes. I chose "Recuerdos de la Alhambra." They could not believe it; I've known this piece since I was 12 years old! They were surprised because they were so used to hearing me play "Bossa in Re"! They just couldn't believe I played classical guitar. I guess after years of playing my own pieces and arrangements, I stopped playing traditional repertory. Anybody who has an ear must understand that to play "Misionera" or "Danza Brasilera" requires classical training.

I believe, with this book, people for the first time will be able to completely appreciate my music and my arrangements because everything is there. I have never had *any* of my music fully notated with the clarity of explanation that is contained within this book. I am pleased!

Jeffrey Herzlich © 2006

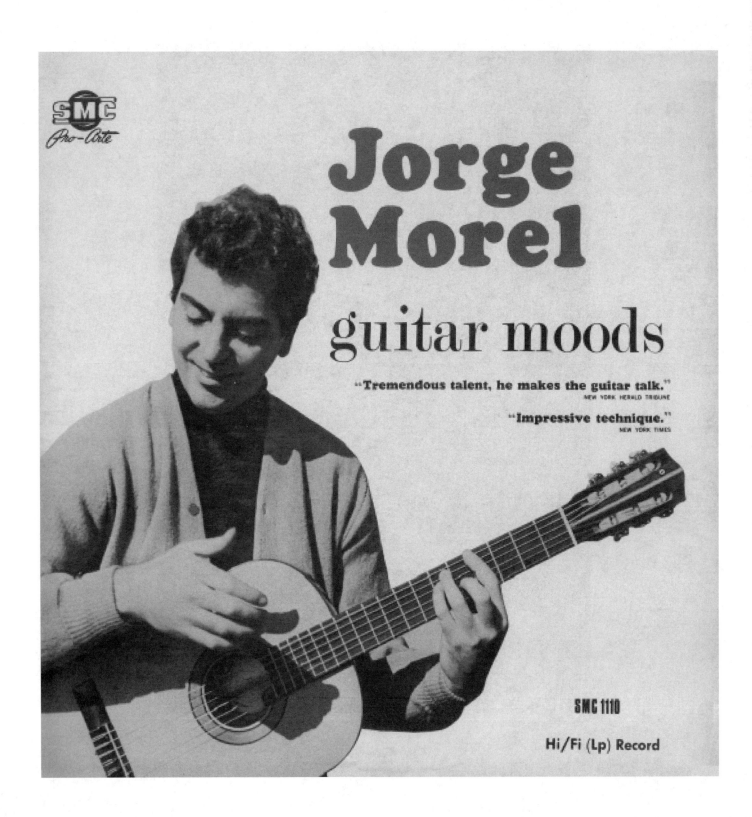

CANCION DEL VIENTO

from *Guitar Moods*
SMC 1110 NY (1966)

TRADITIONAL
ARGENTINEAN LULLABY
arr. JORGE MOREL

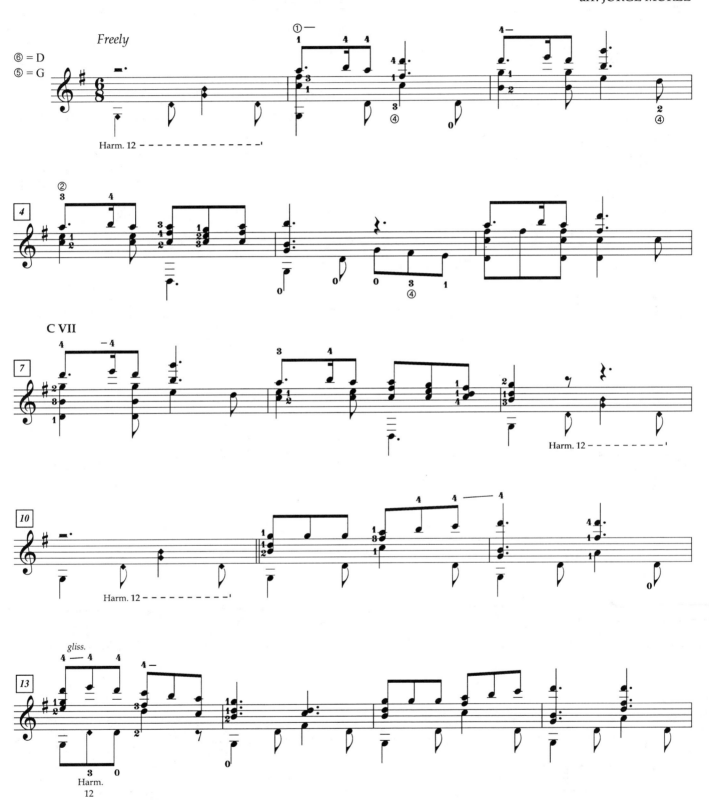

CANCION DEL VIENTO

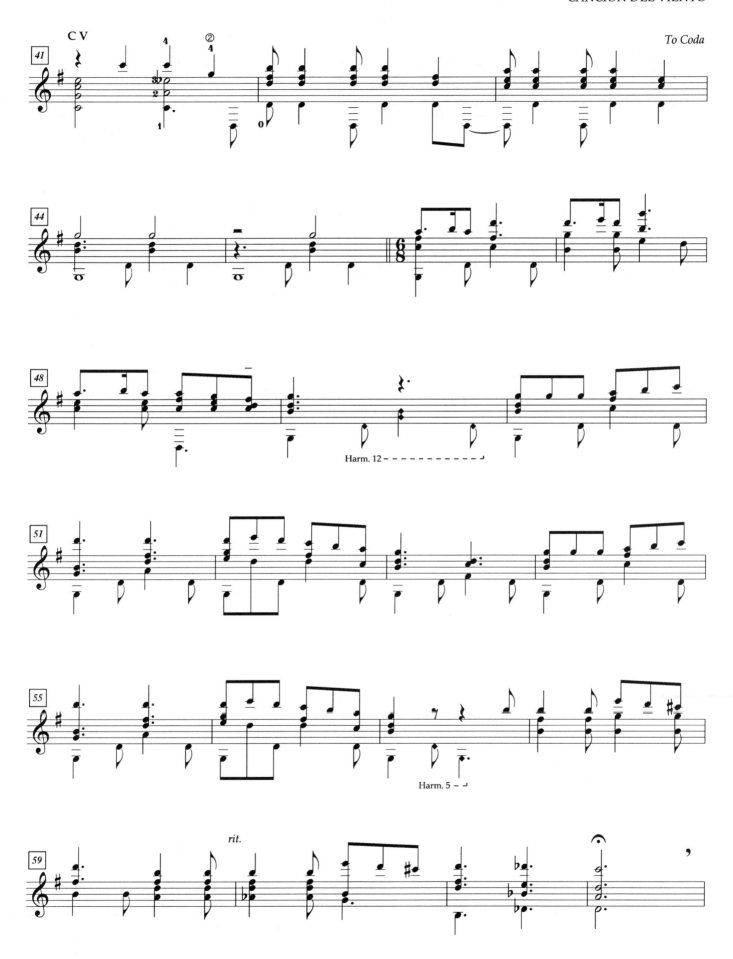

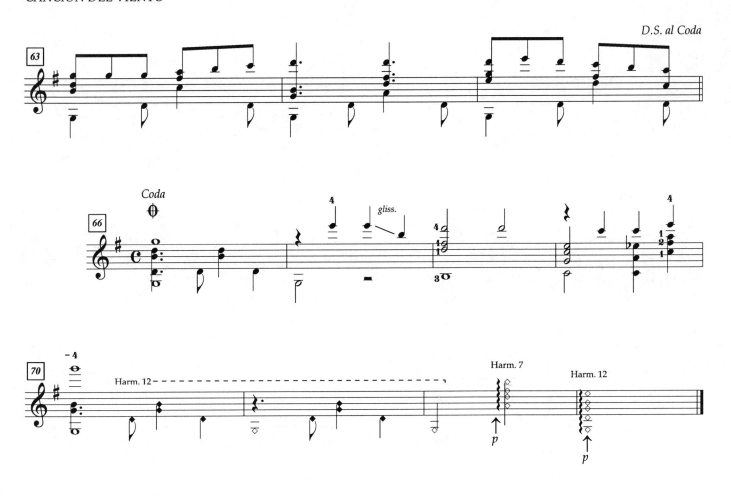

Thoughts about his classic recordings:

"In those days, many of the takes did happen in one shot! I often think, 'How come I can't do that now?' Well, there is a reason for that: it's forty years later!"

Olga and Jorge in New York, 1961.

Before I go to sleep, I kiss Olga's picture. She was a great lady. I loved her and she loved me. She gave me my beautiful daughter. The way she passed away was tragic.

You never get over this. The death of my wife was 33 years ago, on May 16. It is still fresh. That moment was so quick. We didn't even get to the hospital before she died; I will never get over that. I believe that pain, in a way, has helped me create more music. In a radio interview in Argentina, the interviewer said, "Jorge, You told me that you have sadness that you carry throughout your life and that you can never over come it." I said, "I can't!"

I think it is necessary for a composer to be sad sometimes, but that does not mean you have to have a tragedy in your life—it does not have to be like mine, it could be a separation or divorce. If Olga was still alive and we were divorced, that would be a great pain for me to endure. For the creative person in the arts, especially music, this sadness comes through in the music. I wrote the "Cancion" from the *Suite Del Sur* and many other pieces out of sadness. I have also composed a lot of music through happy experiences because I am a happy person.

We must laugh in life. One should take life seriously, of course, but we must laugh, drink good wine, play good music, and remember good things! The time now is so crucial because of what is going on in the world. If you don't feel sadness and compassion for people, then you are not a human being.

In order to experience true happiness, one must also experience deep sadness.

Yes. When Olga died, this is when I started to compose. After she passed, I wrote *Suite Del Sur*. That sad period of my life inspired me to write a lot of music, even many joyful pieces came from that pain. All of a sudden, I remembered those 12 years of marriage and the good times, and I think subconsciously I use these experiences as inspiration.

"As any other guitar fan/enthusiast, when I heard Jorge Morel's recordings I was captivated by his compositions, arrangements, technique and musicality. I met Jorge through a friend and took two lessons. All I wanted to do was learn his excellent 'Take Five' arrangement. Eventually, we became friends and I found out the other side of Jorge: friendly, honest, sincere, unselfish, generous, and a perfect gentleman with integrity.

I consider Jorge my brother, the brother I never had."
—Tony Acosta

"Jorge Morel is the complete guitarist. That is, he possesses a flawless technique, a sound musical ear, an unsurpassed sense of rhythm, and a thorough education in the classical tradition. Of course, these are not the only requisites. One must have ambition and goals. At one time, when he was a child, Jorge must have decided that he was going to be one of the best guitar players in the world.

To my way of thinking he has attained that goal."

—Chet Atkins, 1968

In March of 1973, I went with my wife and my daughter to Nashville while on tour to visit Chet. We went to his house and stayed there for a while. Not long after this, my wife passed away. The following year, I came back to Nashville while on tour, and this is when I gave Chet my guitar.

I was there with a brand new Manuel Velázquez guitar. When Chet heard the guitar he said, "Jorge, I know Velázquez. Oh my God—what a guitar!" He started to play on it and could not put it down. He kept saying, "I love it! I love it!"

I played that guitar for the remaining two or three concerts on the tour, and then returned to Nashville. But before I left, his wife, Leona said, "Jorge, his birthday is next week. I would like to give Chet a guitar just like yours." I said, "I'll talk to Velázquez, but I am afraid he won't be able to build a guitar in one week for Chet." So I said, "I have a Fleta and four or five other guitars, I want Chet to have this guitar for his birthday. Leona, you give it to him, it is yours!" She said, "Jorge, your crazy! He is not going to take it; he is going to want to pay you." I replied, "I don't want any money." I figured he would send me three hundred dollars—I don't know—he wanted to give me something. I said, "Your are not going to pay for that guitar. I will not take your money. You have already given me so much. I am touring with Columbia Artists because of you. This is more meaningful to me than a guitar."

Photo courtesy of the Chet Atkins Trust.

I gave that guitar to Chet because I loved him. And he loved that guitar! You know, I did not care about receiving money for that guitar. Money, money…who cares about money? Money comes and goes, and comes again. You work for money, but it is what destroys friendships. War also…who needs that kind of thing? Because it was for Chet, I was happy for him to have my guitar. I have it back now; Chet's family gave it back to me. I wish I didn't have it, because this would mean Chet would still be with us.

Once, I was in Nashville to play with the Nashville Symphony. I played the *Concierto de Aranjuez* by Rodrigo in an outdoor concert. Chet came to hear me. During another trip to Nashville, Chet said, "I want you to come with me to the Grand Ole Opry for the live performance of the Perry Como Show." He played the Velázquez I gave him.

We got into his Mercedes Benz, a beautiful car, with his partner, Paul Yandell, and as we drove over to the show, we had a flat tire! Chet said, "What are we going to do now? Live television doesn't wait!" I said, "Don't worry, let's get out of the car and I will fix the flat tire." So, I got the tire out of the trunk, and started to change the tire. Chet watched me do this; I did not want him to touch anything for fear of hurting his hands. He had a pair of gloves for me to wear, and I commenced to change the tire by ear. I had never changed a tire before, and Chet was smiling and laughing. He asked, "Have you changed a tire before?" I said, "No!" He nearly fell over laughing! We arrived on time for the show. He told everybody at the Opry about me changing his tire, and my response after the show was, "Chet, I hope we make it back to Nashville on that spare tire."

When Chet would visit New York, he would call me over to his hotel and would introduce me to people he knew. One time I picked him up in my car and we drove to my apartment on Long Island. We had coffee, and we recorded on my reel-to-reel recorder using my microphones. I still have the tape. That tape is a treasure! We played just for fun. He never felt like playing with me, because our styles were so different. I think if we had more time, or I should say if Chet had more time, I think we would have done something together. I wanted to, but I think maybe he felt, "I don't want to ruin this guy."

I remember, in the early 1970s, my wife and I heard the news on the radio that Chet was in the hospital. I called Chet's wife, Leona the next day to see if he was okay. She said he was fine. The operation was a success. Well, thank God he survived all those years after that [*Ed. Note: Chet had colon cancer in 1973*], nearly thirty more years. I feel very sad the cancer came back again; this is how Chet lost his life.

It is hard to find people like Chet Atkins, God bless him! He will be remembered forever, not only as a great guitarist, but also as an artist, a friend, and a wonderful human being who helped so many people—me included!

I would put him on the level of Andres Segovia in his own way. He made the guitar known just as much as Segovia. People don't understand Chet's greatness, but I do. With so many people, if you say Carlos Montoya, they confuse him with Segovia, or confuse Chet with someone like Roy Clark. Don't get me wrong, Roy Clark can play okay, but he is a showman. Chet cared nothing of that. He played music. Chet was the pure artist of the guitar. I love him!

[*Ed. Note: This excerpt was taken from Jorge's interview in* Chet Atkins in Three Dimensions: Fifty Years of Legendary Guitar, Vol. 1 (Mel Bay Publications).]

"Chet was the pure artist of the guitar. I love him!"

I was reading John and Deyan's first book on Chet Atkins [*Chet Atkins in Three Dimensions: Fifty Years of Legendary Guitar*, Mel Bay Publications]. In my interview about Chet from that book, I noticed something I wish to clarify: John asked me if I had met Lenny Breau. I answered, "No, he was involved in things that were not very healthy!" This made it sound like I did not want to meet him. People have since asked me about this. I do not want people to think I am judging him, as I know there are millions of people who suffer addictions. [*Ed. Note: Lenny suffered from drug addiction for most of his creative life.*] The fact is I wish I could have met him because he was a great artist. I have a record Chet gave me of Lenny playing jazz in his basement studio, and I think it is one of the greatest jazz records I have ever heard! I admired him so much and Chet talked about him all the time. When he passed away, I felt terrible!

Maestro Morel 'dons' the thumbpick in honor of his friend, Chet Atkins.

Jorge with Deyan Bratić, 2005.

Yellow Bird

I remember my friend Chet Atkins loved this arrangement. He recorded it for his RCA Victor album, *Class Guitar*.

YELLOW BIRD

from *Guitar Moods*

SMC 1110 NY (1966)

ORTELOU BAYARD

arr. JORGE MOREL

160

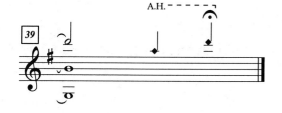

A Note from a Friend

My friend Pepe Romero once asked me,

"Jorge, you are the only guitarist that plays chords like a scale. Instead of playing a single note, you play a group of notes like a scale all together!

How do you do that?"

Dedicated to Rene Izquierdo

SCHERZINO DEL NORTE

JORGE MOREL

SCHERZINO DEL NORTE

SCHERZINO DEL NORTE

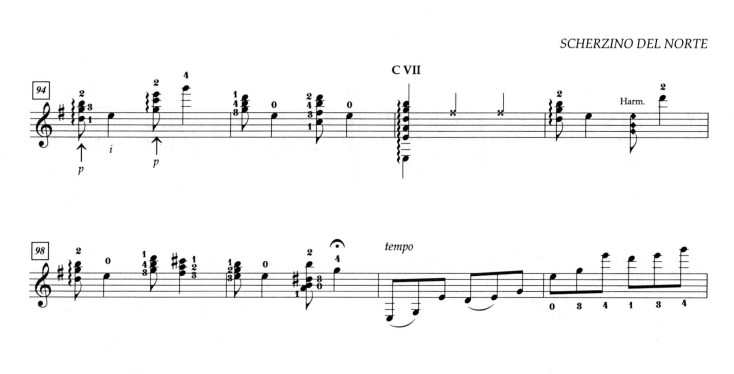

SCHERZINO DEL NORTE

SCHERZINO DEL NORTE

I have many friends in New York, and they are my family: very dear to me. The Bavaro family is very dear to me; Joshua Bavaro is my best student and I am very close to him. Rene Izquierdo and his wife Elina are both wonderful guitarists and Michéle Ramo and his wife, Heidi, also are very dear to me. We meet here in my little place on Saturday nights; we cook and drink wine, listen to music and play concerts for one another. I play sometimes, but I would rather hear them play. We are family as friends because we relate to one another.

Michéle Ramo and wife, Heidi, Jorge, and Thiago DeMello.

Standing left to right: Nato Lima, John Price, Tony Acosta, Carlos Barbosa-Lima, Jorge Caballero, Eddy, Juan De La Mata.
Seated: Elina Chekan, Renee Izquierdo, Jorge Morel.

Ricardo Iznaola and I met a long time ago. He is a great player, arranger and composer—the complete package! He put together a series of festivals called "Guitar Week," and I have been to Colorado twice for this festival. We recently recorded a duet CD that I like very much. I like socializing with people who talk about things other than the guitar, because it gets old when the guitar is all you discuss. Ricardo is a very refined and intelligent man, and it is a great pleasure to be around him.

Left: Jorge socializing with Ricardo Iznaola.

Right: With Barry Mason, Krzysztof Pelech.

Another person who is very special to me is Krzysztof Pelech. I met Krzystof in Poland in 1987, and he plays my music great! From 1987 to 1995, I toured Poland and spent time with Krzysztof and we played many duet concerts together. He is great interpreter of my music and is my friend. Tony Acosta produced a compact disc of him playing my concertos, and it is a beautiful recording.

"I first heard Segovia in 1952.
His 'Sevilla' made me cry."

WHAT CAN BE BAD FOR YOU AT 92 YEARS OLD, MAESTRO?

After his concert at Avery Fisher Hall in 1985, I was invited by Rose Augustine to meet Andrés Segovia for the first time. Thank God he treated me very well! I sat with him and we conversed in Spanish, of course. There were about fifteen people at this little party. Many people wanted to talk to him, but he stayed with me. He said, "Don't worry, I will talk to them later." I was interested in talking to him, and very honored to have shared time with the Maestro.

He was drinking Scotch—he loved Scotch! I was having beer. He leaned over and whispered, "I would like to eat this shrimp—the giant shrimp behind you. Can you get it?" I said,
"But Maestro, of course!"
He said, "Be careful. Don't show it to anybody. Bring it to me like it is for you. My wife does not allow me to eat this."
I asked, "Why not?"
"She says it is bad for me," he answered. I said,
"What can be bad for you at 92 years old, Maestro? Nothing can hurt you!" [*laughs*]

I brought him all he could eat; he was so happy. The Maestro's wife was told by the doctor to restrict his diet; this was why shrimp was off limits. But, he happily ate the shrimp and I hid the evidence from everyone.

Maestro Segovia and Maestro Morel in New York, 1985.

With friend from Radio Nacional,
Sebastian Dominguez in Buenos Aires, 2003.

Dedicated to Sebastian Dominguez

DANZA DE UN RECUERDO

JORGE MOREL

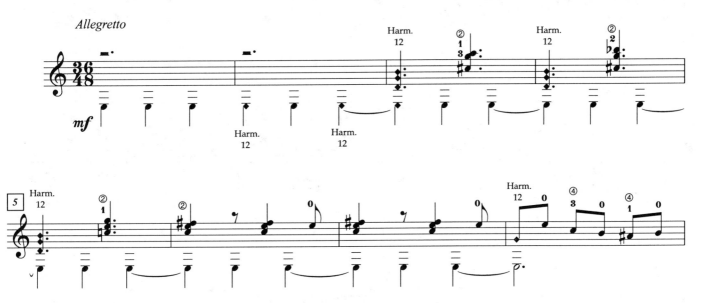

DANZA DE UN RECUERDO

DANZA DE UN RECUERDO

179

Paco de Lucia, Tony Acosta, and Jorge, 1992.

Happy Birthday 2007

Queridísimo Jorge, first of all, happy birthday and congratulations.

All the guitarists of the world thank you for the beautiful music you have given us, both through your playing and, of course, your compositions.

I want to give you a special thanks (Muchas Gracias) from my heart for sharing your music with me so many years ago in London. I learnt so much from you through the spirit of your interpretation, the excitement you transmitted with your performance, and the personality that you gave to your music. You play as you are: honest, warm, friendly, and full of humanity.

I have enjoyed so much playing your music since you first gave me some scores and will continue to play your compositions while I can get my fingers 'round the notes.

With friendship and admiration (Con Cariño),

David Russell
January 2007

GREENSLEEVES

from *Guitar Moods*

SMC 1110 NY (1966)

TRADITIONAL
arr. JORGE MOREL

Jorge with Carlos Barbosa-Lima and Thiago DeMello.

"JORGE MOREL is a most gifted guitarist, composer and arranger. I have had the pleasure and honor of cherishing a wonderful friendship and musical collaboration with him. He truly crosses the boundaries of musical styles, always with the highest standards and refined musical taste. When I fist met him in New York, I was still in my twenties and was impacted by his artistry, virtuosity and musicianship. We have enjoyed pleasant and creative musical experiences together through many years. Jorge also loves life and people, sharing his talent with his friends and encouraging young musicians in the world of music with his experience.

To Jorge, my warmest greetings and abrazos from your friend and colleague that has great admiration for you, looking forward to many years of your musical creativity and friendship." —Carlos Barbosa-Lima

Dedicated to Ana Maria Rosado

CANCION DEL RECUERDO

JORGE MOREL

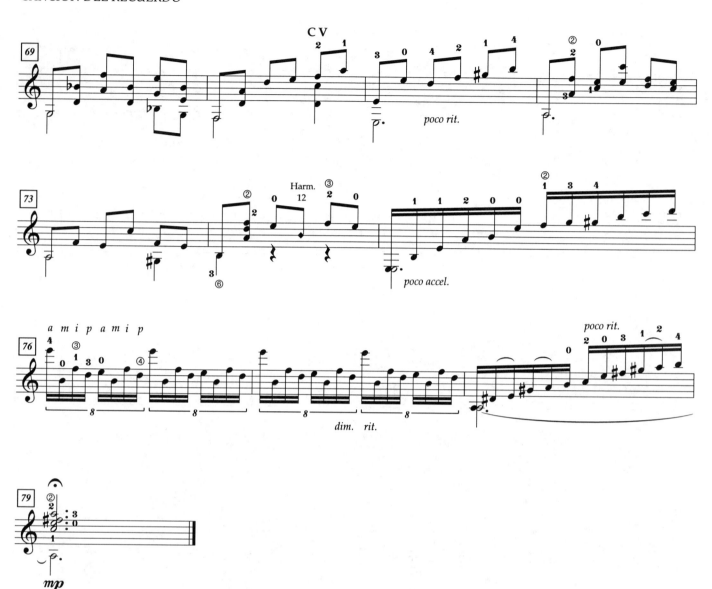

"...*The sound was great but I suffered playing that guitar. It was like playing on a tree!*

...*I had a student who said, 'If you ever want to sell the Ramirez, let me know!' So...I let him know!*"

Photo courtesy of Maurice Summerfield.

An original hand-written manuscript of "Aire de Malambo."

191

Dedicated To Tony Acosta
AIRE DE MALAMBO

JORGE MOREL

AIRE DE MALAMBO

AIRE DE MALAMBO

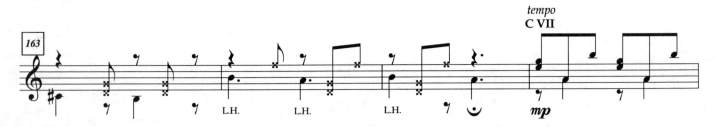

Jorge and friends being serenaded at dinner by the Czech guitarist/composer Štepán Rak.

This is the school where I studied guitar with my first teacher, Amparo Alvariza. She is the reason I play guitar today. I thank her for her great love and admiration and the way she advised my father and mother about my career in music.

My good friend Tony Acosta is here with me.

Buenos Aires
November 2005

Dedicated to Tony Acosta

BRAZILIAN SUNRISE

JORGE MOREL

204

205

With the Assad brothers, 1993.

Dedicated to Eli & Ann Kassner

BARCAROLE

JORGE MOREL

BARCAROLE

210

In Jerusalem, 1991.

Dedicated to Elina Chekan

CAMPANAS

JORGE MOREL

212

CAMPANAS

213

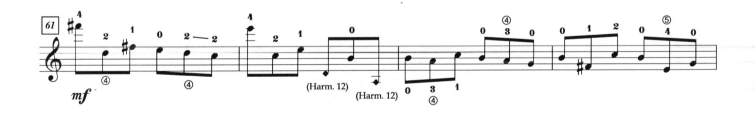

CAMPANAS

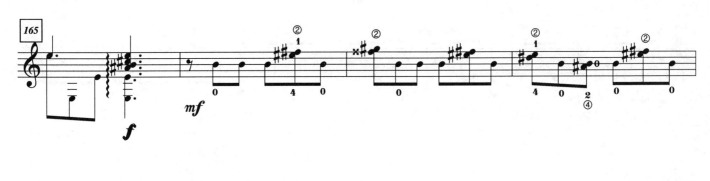

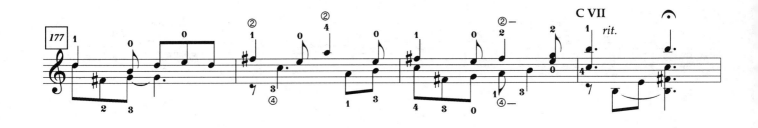

Jorge's dear friend, Rebeca, dancing with son, Jorge.
New York, 1996.

HOMAGE TO A DANCE

Choro

JORGE MOREL

225

SEVILLA

Not content to be an interpreter solely, Jorge Morel sought to forge a distinct sonic signature as a composer for his instrument. This bold, inimitable sound would stretch the fundamental aesthetic of 'classical guitar music,' exploring elements of early American pop, jazz, and Latin folk and dance idioms from various parts of the world. When pondering the combination of these exotic ingredients with a technical facility par excellence (not to mention a prolific output), it is no wonder that parallels are often drawn between Jorge Morel and a preceding Latin American virtuoso, Agustín Barrios.

Unfortunately, the resultant pastiche in Morel's repertoire has eroded his core identity as a *classical guitarist* to many, who ostensibly ignore the instrument he plays—even his technique. To find evidence of this misperception, one familiar with Morel's style needs only to fathom the surprise he has commonly met in his years of touring when heard playing a piece from the standard repertoire. Perhaps a blessing in disguise, the disconnection might reflect the sheer strength of his originality. Nevertheless, it is a peculiar situation in view of Morel's obvious adherence to the guitar's traditions.

With hope of rectifying this anomaly, we have chosen to present Morel's own transcription of "Sevilla" by Issac Albéniz for this book. Introduced to this piece by Segovia, and derived many years ago from the original piano edition, "Sevilla" remains one of Morel's proudest moments in his performing career. By including this gem here, we intend it as a reminder to those who have underestimated his scope as artist of his instrument, the *classical guitar*.

SEVILLA

Sevillanas

ISSAC ALBÉNIZ
TRANS. JORGE MOREL

Allegro moderato

SEVILLA
Sevillanas

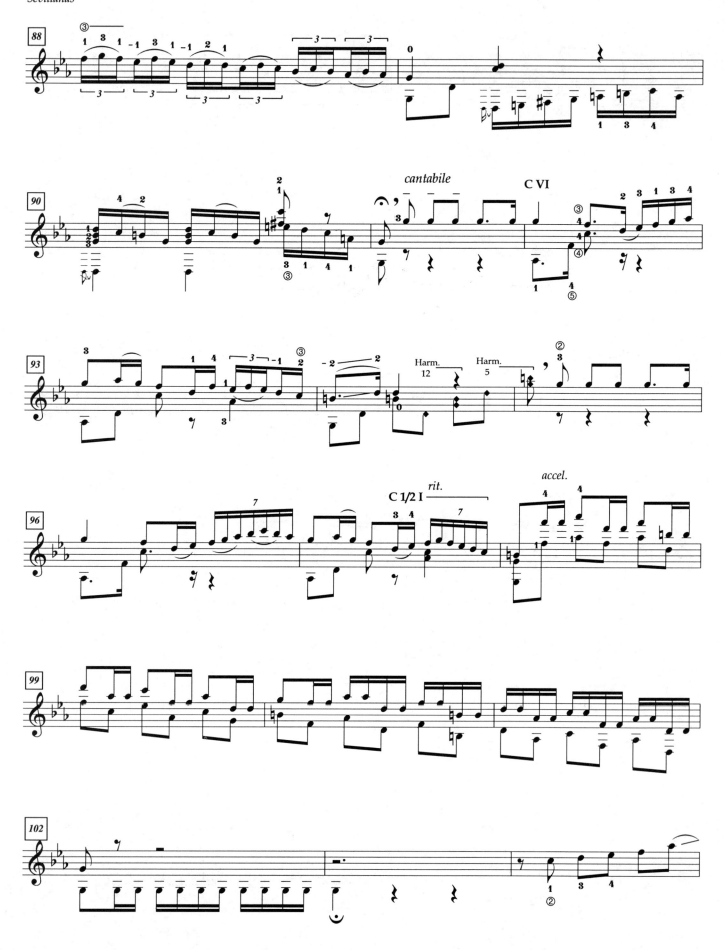

SEVILLA
Sevillanas